VIDEO VERITÉ

AND OTHER STORIES

Copyright © 2010 William Petrick.

All rights reserved. No part of this book may be used or reproduced in any manner whatsoever without prior written consent of the author, except as provided by the United States of America copyright law.

Published by Pearhouse Press, Inc., Pittsburgh, PA 15208
www.pearhousepress.com

First Printing: May 2010

Printed in the United States of America

Library of Congress Control Number: 2009937198

ISBN: 978-0-9802355-3-1

Cover and Book Design: Mike Murray
Author Photo Credit: Andrew Holbrooke

VIDEO VERITÉ

AND OTHER STORIES

WILLIAM PETRICK

PEARHOUSE
PRESS

For Resa Matthews

TABLE OF CONTENTS

Video Verité 1

The Barrens 11

Orange, Texas 21

Car Crazy 33

Crossing Water 47

Sins of the Father 63

Telling Time 77

Turn Around 85

The Perfect View 89

A Woman in Green 99

The Captain 111

Shooting Harlem 127

VIDEO VERITÉ & OTHER STORIES

WILLIAM PETRICK

VIDEO VERITÉ

Ron volunteered to videotape his friends skydiving. He waited exactly seven seconds for the team to free-fall to a maneuvering altitude and join hands. Then he stepped out of the plane, clutching the zoom lens. It was a moment before he discovered he'd jumped without a parachute. It took his friends longer.

The dive team were graduates of a weekend skydiving school. Ron was a video engineer. The night before the jump, he had arranged all the television recording equipment on his extra-firm mattress, sprayed the air with anti-static, and cleaned each component. He also unscrewed the camera casing and checked the microchip board for possible flaws. Finally satisfied, he packed everything into steel reinforced cases for the short ride to the county airport.

The plan to videotape the free-fall had begun as a casual suggestion. They were sitting at a bar near the airport, toasting another successful dive. Someone said they should preserve one of their free-falls on tape—while they were still good. Ron seized on the idea. He could borrow free equipment from the video production company he worked for. Top-quality broadcast equipment, the kind they use on the networks.

Linda, who was also on the jump that day, was the lone dissenter. She wanted a professional to do the videotaping. Someone with experience. But Ron insisted. He knew how to take care of cameras. People paid him well for his skill. The owners of the company respected and trusted him.

"Why did you say that?" Ron asked her later that night as they drove to her apartment." Especially in front of the team. Like I don't know what I'm doing."

"I'm sorry," Linda said. "Really. I wasn't even thinking about that. The video stuff. I was thinking how it would be great for both of us to be in the picture."

"Well then say that," Ron answered, shaking his head.

"I just did." She smiled and hugged his arm.

They signed up for skydiving after Linda found a brochure on free-fall instruction at her health club. It had a color photograph of a young couple, about their age, holding hands in mid-air, somewhere over the Blue Ridge mountains.

Linda didn't remember this until long after the accident. Like the others floating in the windy circle, she watched Ron jump away from the plane, his video camera fastened to his shoulder and the recorder strapped to his stomach. Both of his large hands clung to the camera and he nearly tumbled when the first blast of air hit his knees. But he held on, one hand working the lens focus, aiming the black tube at his friends. They flashed smiles at one another, thrilled to be posing in mid-air.

That's when Ron's chin suddenly snapped upwards like he'd been stabbed in the back. The body inside the flapping jumpsuit stiffened. Only Linda noticed this. Safe in the arm lock of the others, she searched Ron carefully, wary that the camera might slide off and somehow interfere with his parachute pack.

But Ron was no longer trying to focus the camera. He was waving the one arm not held in by the camera. Because he was farther away than they had planned, she thought he was trying to warn them from veering off course. She gave head and touch signals to her partners and everyone peered up through their helmet shields to check Ron's position.

He was off course, far off course. In a glance, they could see he was not trying to videotape them, was not doing anything but clawing at the air, trying to reverse the wind current that pulled him further away. There was no white nylon pack bunched behind his neck. The jumpsuit fluttered from his back like a loose sail.

Linda tried to break away and sent her left side partner spinning on his fiberglass helmet top. Detaching at this altitude too quickly was dangerous and almost always caused collisions. They were falling at high speeds—giving an accidental bump the force of bullet trains meeting head-on.

The other divers, however, managed to restrain Linda even though they could see Ron dropping, about to tumble over himself, his flapping arms already dwarfed by the quiet valley that waited below. Linda kicked at the air, trying to pull away. She screamed; a shriek so piercing that everyone would remember hearing it even though the roar of the winds muffled most human sounds.

Ron saw his friends cling to their safety circle, and spin further away. They seemed to be distancing themselves, trying to keep out of his path. They weren't going to help. He didn't know they were riding another air current, didn't recognize that he and his friends were on separate waves, breaking in opposite directions. He barely even understood what was about to happen to him.

But he had time. He remembered what the instructor had advised if your parachute was damaged or a line got tangled or any of the many things that could and have happened to skydivers. Get your body upright, get your feet first. Landing otherwise, the instructor explained, was like dropping a ripe melon on cement.

That morning, Ron had raced his Mustang to the county airport. It was Sunday and the dark roads were silent and empty. Ron tuned the engine himself for just these kinds of opportunities. The weathered blacktop was wet from a brief night rain and Ron hit the corners like they were banked turns at the speedway. He was strapped into the bucket seat, one hand fused to the steering wheel, the other guiding the stick shift. The engine vibration surged through his hands, up his arms, as he pressed his foot against the gas pedal.

His favorite Sting tune hit stride, pealing out of all four speakers. The cold air rushed through his open window, tingling his neck. The speedometer needle crept silently under the green dashboard light, inching past ninety. He felt the hulking metal body begin to rise, hovering almost weightlessly over the road. The wheels were on the edge of hydroplaning. Ron held at ninety-five, his face flushed, grinning.

"Why are you driving so slow?" Linda had asked once. They were late for a dinner party.

"We'll get there. Don't worry," Ron answered.

"I know we'll get there."

"No way I'm giving all these city drivers the chance for a no-fault collision. They got their insurance. But no insurance is going to help me replace this '65. One of a kind."

Ron felt the speed tightening his stomach. He was tumbling. The wind twisted his bare neck and pinned down his arms and legs. The camera strap had caught inside his shoulder blade and was digging into the joint. Despite the burn that tore through his shoulder, Ron focused on his elbows suspended above him, trying to pull them down, closer to his chest so that he could straighten. Then he could curl himself up for the impact.

The dive team released Linda first. Ron had flown out of view, lost in the growing landscape. It was a country quilt of alfalfa greens and freshly tilled lots. There were tracks of young corn stalks, a chocolate-colored field cut in even blocks, then a dairy farm and silos and trees. A country road slid through it like a lazy black snake.

Linda searched for signs of Ron. But she wouldn't let herself imagine anything. She inspected what was in front of her with all her will. But a sudden, inexplicable panic made her pull on her ripcord too early and she was yanked backwards, laid flat on her back in the invisible air.

She scrambled forward. She couldn't or wouldn't remember what any instructor had told her and she flailed her arms, trying to grab the chute lines. But luck was with her and the wind current itself righted her, and she was swung into her feet-first landing position. She stood in the air now, gulping for breath. Other parachutes appeared on either side of her. Legs dangled from underneath them, some curled, some straight like the stems of white mushrooms. Cars drifted on the uncoiled blacktop. Telephone and electricity lines traced a straight pencil line on one side of the road. There were lush maples, leaves bobbing from the ground breeze.

A grassy field slid into view. Linda stared dumbly at a herd of cows, grazing on a soft, sloping bunker. It was a quiet Sunday morning after all. Anyone might lie in the field and chew on a piece of grass, biding their time.

Linda didn't remember aiming for the landing circle marked with a red windsock or even making a perfect landing, hitting with her feet and immediately going into a roll. She also couldn't recall hearing the heavy thuds on the packed ground as the other members of the team landed safely.

Linda slipped out of her parachute vest and harness and started to run. She ran in the direction she thought Ron must have landed. People have survived falls, she told herself. Ron was ingenious. She could picture his wide grin, explaining in endless, charming detail how he had arrived at the solution. The boyish pride would bring color to his pale face and the bright, dark eyes would search her, gleaning for recognition.

Ron read tech magazines like they were the sports pages. He followed the top electronics companies, studied the published stats of their newest products. Not many people shared his enthusiasm. Once, while he moonlighted in an electronics retail store, a gray-haired man in a crisply tailored suit came into the store to buy a VCR for his daughter. He looked like an intelligent lawyer. Ron was impressed when the man asked questions in precise, well-considered sentences. Not the usual, fumbling customer. The truth was that the bookish man didn't know how to turn on a VCR, make it play, record, reverse and stop. But Ron took the man to be a rare, kindred spirit. All the technical information about video systems that he had absorbed poured out of him. His face was flushed and he spoke without a pause. The lawyer nodded gravely during Ron's lecture, careful to make eye contact. Then he hurried out of the store.

Ron landed on the camera lens and bounced. A few hundred yards later, he bounced off the ground again but not before both legs snapped in half. His crumpled body spun playfully in the air one more time before he slammed on his back, the bones breaking in his back like dry twigs. One of his lungs collapsed and blood rushed out of his open mouth. Remarkably, his neck and skull remained in one piece inside his shattered helmet.

Ron knew none of this. He had lost consciousness long before impact. In the midst of trying to bring his arms into his chest, he had made the mistake of glancing at the ground. It was huge, inescapable and roaring toward him faster than he'd seen anything move in his life.

The videotape was in one piece. The recording unit, which had been taped to his stomach and was shattered by the impact, protected the cassette. Linda refused to watch it or know what it recorded for posterity. Fearfully, she remembered her first instinct, the queer suspicion that had compelled her to want someone else to do the taping. She was afraid for him. But she had ignored the warnings, not daring to hinder him and had let Ron rush on with his scheme, the little suggestion that had swelled into a major production and then, against all common sense, conspired to jeopardize his own safety. All for what?

A week after the accident, the dive team arranged to watch the tape. They sat in a circle around the extra-large screen and joked nervously while the tape was re-wound. At the same time, they monitored the sounds of the neighborhood; the distant hedge trimmer, the squeal of kids happily at play, the sudden rush of a passing car. At any minute, someone could knock on the door or ring the telephone and they would be found out.

When the tape clanked into forward, bright color bars and a loud, piercing audio test-tone appeared. The team's other concerns vanished. The men gradually, almost imperceptibly, sank into a meek solemnness. They inched closer to the screen and each other. Their healthy, young faces mirrored the same steady, electronic blue.

The first shot was a picture of the Cherokee VI they had flown in. It was a sleek, late-model plane. The grass underneath it was still wet with dew and, through the video lens, flashed like pieces of glass. The camera panned away to show the long airfield and the squat, black control tower that was planted midway down the freshly-mowed grass.

They had seen the Cumberland County Airport many times. But the dive team studied the big screen as if they'd never experienced such an unusual landscape. It was more than the unseen friend who directed the camera. It was as if they had been granted some extraordinary privilege.

A young woman stepped into camera view. She was as tall as a man, big-boned, with a long easy gait. Her thin figure was hidden by the jumpsuit and she had a parachute pack slung over one shoulder. She held Styrofoam coffee cups in each large hand. The faint steam rose off the open tops and brushed her long, bare neck.

Linda grinned when she got closer and the lens framed her in a close-up. The brilliant morning light lit her chestnut hair from behind like a movie star's. But it created too strong a contrast for the camera and caused much of her face to be lost in shadow. But her sharp, intelligent eyes caught the ambient light at the last moment and made her seem more mysterious and alluring. There was a playful smile in them, a look once meant only for Ron.

The team was next. They were videotaped walking to the plane, all in the same yellow jumpsuits, waving before they stepped inside. Any other time, this image might have been good for some mocking remarks or at least a chuckle. But the team watched the scene dully, waiting patiently the way a movie audience might tolerate a slow part in an action film.

The next scene brought a reaction. It began with the open door of the plane. One yellow suit after another came to the doorway, then shot out into the white light. Then the camera moved to the door and, for one instant, almost a flash, it passed by a parachute pack that leaned next to the door.

The picture struggled for focus, first on the door edge and then out toward the passing clouds. The lens iris adjusted and found blue sky. The image suddenly zoomed forward. The valley was a huge, formless gray. The camera moved in a quick circle and then found the yellow jumpsuits. The picture shook violently, then held an even, graceful image of four people, suspended in air like children on a playground turnstile.

The picture jerked up, then over to the side and up and again. They were quick, sharp staccato movements. The angle and width of the image increased. It could have been a zoom out. But then it jerked upwards, pointing at the smooth sheet of blue. It became a still shot. Nothing but clear, empty sky. Silent. Then the picture did a strange thing. It spun through the sky, almost like a special effect. There was no mistaking the sense of flying; the sense of the weightlessness, the wonder of swooping through the cool air. The image continued its buoyant glide until it caught a corner of the green valley. The corner spread across the extra-wide screen. The land was in soft focus, zooming toward the camera. There was a silo, cows, a brown field. The field hurled itself at the camera. No one looked away. The speaker exploded with the harsh crackle of blank, amplified sound. The team gawked at the screen, scratched with electronic snow.

One diver finally released himself and snapped off the power. Like everyone else in the room, the still quiet freed him. He went back and dropped into his seat. Sharp, quick exhalations pierced the air around him. A high, boyish voice muttered "Jesus," then lapsed into the tense silence.

The dive team gave the videotape to Ron's mother. They were careful to explain that her son had lost his life bravely, striving to create something lasting. His tired, silent mother smiled and set the tape with Ron's other mementos gathering dust in his old room. The dive team watched her shuffle to the bedroom with the same rapt attention they had given to the television screen. Years later, they would remember that moment as much as the video itself. Her tired, indifferent walk became an accusation. They felt childish and irresponsible. They should never have let him try it. They knew it was dangerous.

One early Sunday morning, years later, Linda drove back to the little airport. She was dating someone she wasn't in love with and had awakened thinking of Ron. It had been triggered by a remark that her boyfriend had made the night before. He was telling a story about a female mountain-climber who had fallen off a ninety-foot ledge and survived. She had been taking stunt lessons from a professional stunt man and knew how to land.

Linda drove fast along the road, as she was certain Ron did. She pictured his long, sharp profile and that small, nearly imperceptible smile. The machine's performance made him more confident, more satisfied with the world around him.

"Can you feel it?" he demanded." That's more than a few pistons firing. That's perfection. It's got a life of its own."

Linda grinned now as she had then, sharing his passion for the moment. It was the side of him she loved the most; the charged, intensely focused energy. He seemed as strong and fearless as his technology. And yet there was a part of her that felt compelled to protect him, sensing intuitively that the confidence he held was fragile, could break down at any moment. He was like a young boy trying to climb a tree, concentrating on the form and structure of the limbs, not for a moment suspecting the branches wouldn't hold him.

Ron had not died instantly. The fall had shattered his body and flung him to the side of the field like a stray piece of litter. He laid in his own darkness, his head exploding in white, blinding flashes from the pain. Still, he held on, trying to pull his mind out of it, struggling to think. He'd been in pain before and he'd outlasted it. So he scrambled harder, willing it to end. But the burning, searing flashes were relentless. One after the other, boring into him, screeching from every corner. He couldn't see, couldn't hope to see and then the shock kicked into him and, in his mind, he screamed, but still he held on, unwilling, unable to quit.

It was over an hour before the dive team found him. No one, not even Linda, had the courage to get near him. His body was crumpled and twisted. The fiberglass helmet was splintered but managed to preserve his face. Linda clung to the warm, breathing body next to her and closed her eyes, willing what she saw forever out of her memory. She could not, would not remember Ron this way.

There were times when she had no choice. But now, as she strolled along the airfield, she remembered him that Sunday, waving to her through the blue darkness from behind the camera. He was tinkering with the color adjustments and kept his hands in place even after she leaned over to kiss him good morning.

"I hope you didn't sleep with that thing, too," she said.

"There's no moving parts in these new chip cameras," Ron said, grinning.

"I'll get some coffee," Linda answered and slipped the pack higher on her shoulder. Just as she was about to reach the entrance to the hanger, Ron yelled to her. She turned to face him but couldn't hear what he was trying to say. He had stepped away from the camera and tripod and was pointing to the sun that had climbed over the hills and spread a sheet of pale gold over the quiet airfield.

"Hold that thought," she yelled, wanting to run to him, to capture and hold with him the unexpected beauty of the moment. A snapshot of happiness. But already he was crouched behind the camera, squinting through the viewfinder, recording the beginning of the day for another time.

The Barrens

Julie watched the fat cop swagger up to their rental car, his stout belly leading the way like he was carrying a watermelon. The police dispatch radio squawked into the hot, silent swamp that surrounded them. It was the middle of July, a muggy weekend, when most people escaped to the seashore or the mountains.

"You know you run a stop sign back there?" the cop said, his ferret eyes peering at Matt, then darting to the empty backseat, looking for clues. At the last moment, he found Julie, his gaze jumping from her red bikini top to her matching lips. She smiled, his hungry look reminding her of another big cop, years ago, his eyes feasting on her as she cowered in the rear seat of his cruiser.

"We haven't passed a car for miles," Matt said, as if he was about to begin one of his summations.

"No. Don't expect you'd see a lot of cars," the cop said, nodding.

"That's why I just slowed down. There was no reason to stop. No cars coming," Matt continued. His tone of voice had turned conspiratorial, and Julie waited for him to reveal that he was an assistant DA in the city. Law enforcement. They were in the same business.

"A stop sign means stop," the cop said. He looked the car up and down as though it might fit the description of a stolen vehicle. Then he asked for license and registration.

"This a rental," the cop said, reading the yellow Hertz form. "You drive here all the way from New York?"

"We just came to see the Pine Barrens," Matt said. "Heard a lot about it."

The cop laughed, a loud, good-natured laugh that shook his watermelon belly and burst through his flushed cheeks. His eyes watered as he opened them to regard the young couple as if for the first time.

"People usually try to avoid the place," the cop said. "'Specially now, in summer. The bugs are mean. Chiggers, masquits, everything."

"We like swamps," Julie said. She pretended to adjust one of her red straps.

The cop adjusted his tan cap. Sweat beaded on his wide, slightly reddened forehead. He remained silent, studying the ground at his feet as though it were a puzzle.

"I'm gonna go run a little check," the cop said finally. As he waddled back to his patrol car, Julie sank into her unblemished seat and giggled.

"We like swamps?" Matt said.

Julie grabbed a few silken bangs of hair and studied them in the harsh, midday light. "This was your idea, I recall," she said, glancing at him through her veil of fine, tawny hair.

Matt nodded and pursed his lips in a way that made him look like a schoolboy instead of a grown man.

"The Pine Barrens," Julie said, sitting up in her seat. "Somewhere we had never been to before." A clean slate, she wanted to add but didn't.

Matt looked for the cop in his side mirror.

"It could be worse, I guess," Julie said.

"How's that?"

"I'm not sure. But I'll get back to you."

Julie laughed at herself, feeling sad and reckless at the same time. She knew they had made a mistake coming here, knew long before they had left her apartment in the West Village.

"Let's see," Matt said. "The air-conditioning doesn't work, there isn't a restaurant within sixty miles of this place—if we had the gas to get there—and we don't even know where we are exactly."

"You forgot the huge ticket from the cop," Julie said.

"Right," Matt said.

They sat in the hot silence of the car. Cicadas buzzed furiously outside the window. The pine trees and scattered brush were bleached a pale, sickly green by the midday sun.

"Maybe we can just go for a long hike," Matt suggested. "Have a picnic."

"Splendor in the swamp?"

"I'm just trying to make the best of it," Matt said.

Julie looked at her nails, noting that she was past due on a manicure. She loved being pampered at the New Age salon where a manicure/pedicure also included a foot massage. She's always left feeling refreshed and clean. A new person.

"The guidebook said there are great hikes in the shade of the trees," Matt continued. "We just have to get oriented to where we are exactly, and then we can find the trailheads. Maybe the cop knows."

"Didn't he just say this place was full of chiggers—what is a chigger anyway?"

"This is the wilderness, Julie."

"I thought it was New Jersey."

A year ago, Julie thought, they would have been happy to be anywhere so long as they were together. On any lazy Saturday like this one, they would have been finding any old place and the time to take off their clothes and make love for as long as their bodies could hold out.

"Maybe we should just go back," Julie said. "Cut our losses."

The statement unexpectedly chilled them both. The awkward silence that followed was impervious even to the buzz saw of cicadas.

"I think we should stay," Matt said, staring out the front window.

Julie studied her boyfriend's handsome profile. The forehead, the delicate eyebrows that women coveted, the aquiline nose, the sculptural cut of his chin. Matt had always been pretty to look at, and his boyish earnestness to please her had long been a charm. But at this moment she wanted and needed someone older, someone to take control of the situation. She no longer desired an equal.

"Can we have some air-conditioning?" Julie asked. She reached under her hair and wiped away the sweat that pooled at the nape of her neck.

"He's going to be back in a minute," Matt said.

"So?"

"Then we can turn on the car."

"Are we trying to save fuel?" Matt, she had often noticed with annoyance, harbored those New England genes that made frugality almost an instinct.

"No. I just think turning on the car could alarm the cop."

"You're worried about him?"

"I just don't want to make things worse."

Julie's hand was on the door rest and pulling on the latch before she even was aware of what she was doing. In the next moment, she was stepping out of the car.

"What are you doing?" Matt demanded.

Julie waved away the gnats that immediately swirled around her face. The heat bore into her even though the sun had momentarily slipped behind a passing cloud. The empty road looked equally forlorn in both directions. Nothing but bugs and heat and misery.

"Damn it, Julie," Matt suddenly said. "What are you doing? You're going to provoke that cop."

Julie smiled without answering. She strolled around the car until she was standing in the middle of the street. There were only two ways to go. She checked her clothes and was annoyed to see that there were faint marks where her panties touched her white cotton clamdiggers.

"Julie," Matt pleaded.

"Bye-bye," she said.

Julie felt the cop's narrowed eyes on her long before she met them. Most men rarely turned down an opportunity to watch her sinuous, sauntering gait, and the cop was no exception. She was amused by the attention and liked the brief, if fleeting burst of power it gave her. He wasn't the first cop to consider coming on to her. But he said nothing until she was almost past the patrol car.

"You best get back in the car, ma'am," he said. The police radio crackled with a report of a crime in progress. Julie slowed, glancing coyly over her shoulder like a runway model and smiled for her hapless fan.

"I have to pee so bad," she said. "But I'll be right back. Promise."

Julie continued on until she reached the edge of the swamp. She expected to hear another warning from the watermelon cop or even the heavy clomping of his black boots on the empty road. But only his CB radio spoke, rattling off police codes for a distant crime or infraction.

"Julie!" Matt's voice grated on her. "Are you out of your mind?"

Matt was so…straight, she concluded. This was the single trait that continued to annoy and sadden her. The world was an essentially rational place for Matthew, where the most trying struggle was finding a mate and making detailed five-year career plans. He knew little about that other world, the one she had inhabited since she was a fifth-grader, where neither love nor security nor sanity was assured. She had never told him the truth about her first years in New York, either, knowing he would either pity her or be repulsed by the life she had lived for a time. But he wouldn't understand, not really. Even she had trouble accepting how low she had sunk.

"Get back in your car, mister. Now." The cop's voice bellowed over the swamp like the croak of a beast on the African savannah.

"I was just calling to my girlfriend, for Christ's sake."

"Get back inside."

"She's troubled," Matt pleaded.

"I'm troubled?" Julie thought to herself. "I'm troubled?"

"Stop where you are," the cop roared.

"Hey, hey…" Matt said, his voice thin with sudden fear. "There's no need for that."

Julie felt a sudden, unexpected burst of hope. She could just walk away from things and start over. There was no need to work things out as Matt urged, no need to revive something that had long since died. Life was too short to rectify abject failures. The thing was just to move on, to leave the past behind. Like the pilgrims. You just pack and move to a new world and start over.

"Put your hands up on the roof," the cop ordered.

"What? What are you talking about?"

"Now. I want 'em up there now."

"OK, OK," Matt responded. "This is crazy."

"I don't know what you and your girlfriend are trying to pull, but I ain't havin' none of it. Hear me?"

"Pull? We're not trying to do anything."

"Don't turn around. I want to see your hands on the car, mister."

"The roof is hot as a skillet," Matt said.

"Put them up there."

Julie stopped. A loose, gravel path led through the bush to a slow moving stream. The water was the color of urine, but there were a few stray evergreens that gave off a pleasing mountainlike scent. Julie crouched down on the gravel, intending to examine the gurgling water more closely. But instead, the feel and sound of loose gravel under her feet took her mind back a decade ago. It was coal-black gravel then, and the air was cool with autumn. She was crouching alongside the tracks of the railroad, waiting. She had left home, crying, but realized too late that she had nowhere to go. She was thirteen and her mother was in California or Chicago or Canada. No one, not even Dad, really knew. It had been a year almost to the day when she had sat the family down in the living room and announced she was leaving. "I'm in love," she had said. "I'm in love, and I want to live with him." And then her mother was gone.

The hard, sharp closing of a car trunk issued like a rifle report. Julie stood up quickly, looking back in the direction of Matt and the cop. But the squat bushes and weeds obscured her view. She remained still, listening and more curious than alarmed.

"What's this?" the cop asked.

"What do you think?"

"Don't get smart ass with me, mister."

"It's a picnic basket."

"What's in it?"

"Food, water, wine…a picnic. A picnic."

An all too familiar fear trickled through Julie like ice water. At the last moment, before Matt had come back inside her apartment to pick up the Williams-Sonoma picnic basket, she had slipped a small, half-filled sandwich bag inside underneath the napkins. Matt usually didn't get high, but, on occasion, he would surprise her and join in. She had hoped this trip might be one of those happier times.

"Take it apart," the cop said.

"What?" Matt said. "Isn't this going just a little too far?"

"I said take it apart."

"I assume you have probable cause?" Matt said in his courtroom voice.

Julie giggled nervously. The past was all coming back to her. The leer of the burly cop, the way he appraised her with a mix of lust and disgust as if she were a common whore and junkie. She had been behind the locked door of that short stay hotel room when a short, Italian undercover cop bounded into the room with shards of rotted wood at his feet, finding her on her knees, the coke dealer standing, his designer trousers at his ankles. There was a crack pipe at the edge of the bed, and the room smelled like lighter fluid. The bad old days when a fix trumped everything.

"This is Brie from Zabar's," Matt was saying. "The pate is from a great little French shop in the village. And the wine is Pouilly-Fuisse, a white Burgundy. Satisfied?"

While her boyfriend's voice remained level and calm, Julie felt the bite of his sarcasm, a clear warning that Matt was pissed.

"Take everythin' out."

"It's silverware and glasses and napkins. Very expensive."

"Take it out."

Julie recognized the ensuing silence between the two men. How strange men were when it came to communicating most feelings, even simple surprise. Words, language that expressed passing emotions, were suspect at best. Even Matthew, who was educated and articulate, could turn mute in the face of strong emotions.

"You gonna tell me that's dessert?" the cop said.

"I honestly don't know…" Matt began but stopped.

"Slowly, real slowly," the cop instructed, "I want you to put your hands behind your back."

The metallic jingle of the handcuffs frightened Julie. She searched the surrounding barrens behind her, prepared to run or hide or both. They shouldn't have come here. She shouldn't have listened to Matthew. They should have quit while they were ahead. It was foolish to think they could return to the innocence of the beginning when they were both drunk with infatuation and lust, drawn together in spite of their apparent differences.

"OK, Missie," the cop called. "Time's up."

Julie could not move or speak. Without warning, she felt the tear on her cheekbone, sliding down her cheek. She waited until it was on her chin, well clear of her makeup, before she wiped it away. There was nowhere to go.

Out of the shade, the sun was fierce. It pricked her face and scalp as she marched up the dirt road toward the men. They waited by the car, watching. Julie bit hard on her lower lip when she met Matthew's furious gaze, his wrists handcuffed behind him like a common criminal.

"Nice work, Julie," Matt snapped.

She stared out the window as the patrol car rumbled along the dirt road. Puffs of dirt swirled in their wake. Julie was struck with how vast the wilderness seemed. No matter how far they drove or what turn they made, there were simply more thickets of the evergreens that Matt had described as dwarf pines. There were no telephone lines, no cell towers, no distant homes or buildings. There was only the forest as it was probably thousands of years ago.

"What a mess," Matthew said, finally, his voice now subdued.

"At least we don't have to call a lawyer," Julie said, glancing away from the window.

Matthew did not smile or even acknowledge her wisecrack. He stared ahead as though she were not even in the car. The sudden, lengthening distance between them terrified her. She was being left behind. It was her doing, she knew. Everything she had done had been reckless and stupid. She was more than troubled, she knew. She was broken, and, in the end, broken is broken.

"I'm sorry, Matthew," she said suddenly, willing herself not to cry. "I really wasn't thinking."

Matthew continued to stare ahead, cold, silent, and remote. On the other side of the Plexiglas, the cop's pink neck bulged over his collar. Julie felt nauseated.

"We shouldn't have come. It was a mistake." Julie spoke to passing trees. The radio squawked from the front seat.

"No it wasn't," Matthew said, so quickly it startled her. She turned to look at him, expecting an explanation.

"I know you're angry, but can you at least look at me? Tell me why we came all the way out here to these Pine Barrens?"

"You know why, Julie."

Matthew's face was taut, his jaw fixed. But there was a halting shyness about him, a quiet boyishness that awed her.

"Tell me," Julie said. But she could not summon her usual wisecrack self. In fact, she was sorry she had spoken at all.

"Tell you," Matthew repeated, full of hesitancy. "OK. I'll tell you. I love you. That's why I wanted to come. OK?"

Matthew's anger confused her. How could he know what he was saying? He didn't know what love was. He didn't know who she really was, so how could he love her? How?

At the last moment, she caught the cop's seed-black eyes watching her in the rearview mirror. They were hard, impenetrable eyes that seemed buried inside his fleshy face like black dots.

"It's my pot," Julie said, finally. "I put it in there. He didn't know."

"Don't matter," the cop said, returning his attention to the road ahead of them. "Don't matter at all."

"I just confessed, damn it to hell," Julie said. "He doesn't need to be involved. I don't want him involved. It was me. Me, me, me. I screwed up."

"It's OK, Julie," Matt said.

"No, it's not," she said, feeling weak with fear, knowing what was likely to happen when they reached the police station and were booked and her old record appeared. It wasn't going to be OK, then.

"We're going to be fine," Matt continued in a quiet, trusting voice.

"We're going to jail, Matt."

"I'm aware of that," her boyfriend said. "I'm aware of that."

"Just checking," Julie said. The road ahead turned onto a major asphalt highway, and suddenly, it seemed to her, there was traffic everywhere like angry yellow jackets darting in and out of sun. They were out of the Barrens, but it still felt like the middle of nowhere.

Orange, Texas

This happened on the way to New Orleans. Will was hitching along the Gulf Coast, relieved to be out of the Sally and back roaming as he pleased. He'd caught a ride with another Northerner who drove a boat-sized Buick, one of those old, indestructible freighters that seemed to float at highway speed. The gaunt, ex-hippie driver gabbed for miles then abruptly interrupted himself and offered Will a nibble of acid.

"Just chew until it's all gone," the ex-hippie instructed when Will spent too long observing the fleck of paper stuck to his thumb. "Don't worry, kid. It ain't enough for psychedelics."

"So you were saying you worked the oil rigs," Will said, anxious to change the subject. He tried to grind the paper between his teeth but it kept slipping off and sticking to his gum, which he feared might affect how the drug worked. He sneaked a sidelong glance to see if the driver was watching.

"Oh yeah," the ex-hippie said, swallowing his hit. It was a much larger dose than he had given Will.

"Like I was tellin' you, the rigs were boredom. Big time. They choppered you in and out of these wild west towns between shifts." He flicked his round, stubbled chin at the concrete bungalows that drifted toward them. They were boarded up, the slats whitened by years of exposure.

"But you made serious greenback out there, in the middle of that."

The ex-hippie sneered at the aluminum water that stretched to the horizon. "Most hung in for a year then disappeared."

Will felt a rush, and his mind flashed with a filmlike image of troops of gaunt ex-hippies storming in on Hueys. The machines chugged and whistled out of the low clouds, their tails tilted to the ground like praying mantis drifting down to a nest in the marshland.

"How long did you last?" Will asked.

"Stuck out one shift. Being out there where you can't see land, livin' with 50 horny guys was not my idea of the good life. Know what I mean?"

"No girl friends?" Will asked. "All that time?"

"There were whores, kid," the ex-hippie said, shaking his head. "But that didn't help. Not out there. Not in the middle of all that nothing. Nothing to do but get sick of yourself."

Will nodded as if he understood. But he thought about his girlfriend back in Maryland, remembering the sweet smell of her skin, the smooth legs, the very beginning when they made love all the time and never wanted to stop. It already seemed like another lifetime.

"You ever been out there in the middle of the Gulf, kid?"

"Yeah," Will said, about to elaborate but the ex-hippie cut him off.

"They don't make strong enough LSD to stick me back on top of the floating lunatic asylum. Lotta guys went nuts out there. Seen one crazy Cherokee jump from the tower like he was gonna take a swim. Last war cry we heard from him."

"It was different for me," Will said, folding his arms.

"How's that kid?"

"I like it out there. It's peaceful out in the Gulf. You can think about things. I was working on a fishing boat and I'd still be on that damn boat if I wasn't having to deal with sleeping in the Salvation Army hostel. The bums there call it Sally. But it smelled like a frat house the morning after. A real pigsty."

The ex-hippie stared through the dirty windshield. His bony hands gripped the black, oversized steering wheel. He glanced at the smudged dashboard long enough for Will to understand that the gas gauge was being examined.

"You got a few bucks you can chip for gas, maybe? I know I've got enough to get us through a few towns but we'll be short going all the way to New Orleans."

"I'm a little short myself," Will lied. He wasn't hitchhiking to save money but he felt it violated some unwritten law of the road to pay anything if you were thumbing.

"Well," the ex-hippie said, sounding rehearsed. "Maybe we'll be OK. This car does real good on mileage if you know how to drive her."

By mid-afternoon surface pipes began to appear along the roadside and Will tracked them to the refineries that loomed ahead. The gnarled tubing and the cotton white smoke spewing from the stacks reminded him of industrial New Jersey, the bleak, colorless stretch along the turnpike. But it didn't smell like sulfur here. The muggy air held the scent of brine and sun-dried sargasso.

The refineries were soon absorbed by the vast marshland. The soft grasses stretched for miles, waving like a woman's hair in the slight breeze off the Gulf. Will searched the horizon, remembering the fishing boat. They had gone about ten miles offshore where the water turns translucent green and schools of white and silver fish flashed by like bright coins. The captain had taught him how to tie different knots and use the spear hook to stab the red snappers and the blunt-nosed sharks that the fishermen-tourists struggled to reel onto the deck. He was feeling like part of the crew, part of a community of sorts, and he was able to forget about home, about his past, about whatever it was he was doing, wherever he was going.

"Orange, Texas," the ex-hippie cried out as they passed a "Welcome to Orange" sign. Will spotted the shopping mall first. The sprawling monolith gleamed ahead, new and bland like the one just built near his parents' home. The developers had created it by filling in a spring-fed pond where Will and his boyhood friends went exploring. A parking lot had replaced the tall grasses that had once hid the dark green sanctuary from the distant highway.

"Pretty upscale," the ex-hippie warned even as they entered a cheap strip lined with gas stations and a Dunkin Donuts. "Gas'll cost us in this ville."

Cars crept near the mall's entrance, shopping for parking spots. A blue Honda inched along the perimeter, clearly anxious to find a yellow box closest to the aluminum arches spanning the glass entrance. It reminded Will of his father, endlessly hunting for a close-in spot, anxious to avoid a more distant parking place as if walking were some kind of indignity, a chore to be avoided at all costs. Will didn't ever want to go back to that kind of life, the shopping malls, the mind numbing routines, the frightening, insidious boredom that paved every road.

The traffic light ahead flashed amber. Even as it changed to red, the Buick continued to coast along, unconcerned. Will hated people who slammed on their breaks at the last minute, screeching tires. He was about to protest to the ex-hippie when he noticed the drug induced stare. He wasn't waiting for the last possible moment to stop. He wasn't even thinking about it. He was traveling somewhere else.

Will felt more than actually saw the red light that drifted toward him. As the dangling traffic light swept out of view, he was startled by the sudden quiet. They sailed through the intersection as effortlessly as the fishing boat had plowed the Gulf. Will felt so calm, calmer than he could ever remember feeling. The car was slowing down, he thought. The ex-hippie had just wanted to unnerve him.

It was then that the green station wagon, green as a melon, showed its broadside. A man about his father's age had not yet turned to greet them. When he did, his thick black cartoon eyebrows narrowed. The cars slammed into each other at full speed.

Will was yanked backward, metal screeching in his ears. The windshield shot at his face, too fast for his arms to react. It knuckle-punched his nose, slammed his forehead. And then everything stopped.

In the stillness that followed, Will examined the cracked window and tasted the warm blood dripping across his lips. The traffic noise, the engine, the radio tuned to rock and roll, all of which had seemed to vanish before, now roared back to life as if someone had patched in a sound board.

"Aw, man," the ex-hippie said, gingerly testing the cracked windshield. "This is bad. Real bad."

"There's not a scratch on you," Will said, licking his lips.

"I don't have insurance, kid."

Will had a sudden, uncomfortable thought.

"You own this, don't you?" Will asked.

"It's in the family," the ex-hippie answered.

"Does this family of yours know you got it?"

The flashing lights of a squad car appeared in the intersection. Will stepped out of the car, anxious to escape, to separate himself from whatever trouble the ex-hippie was about to bring upon himself. But as soon as Will stood on the asphalt, he had to steady himself on the hot metal hood. Instead of walking away, he clung to the car hood, watching the two Texas cops in desert khaki emerge from under the candy blue lights. The man with the bushy eyebrows, who had been driving the station wagon, strolled over to meet them. The three men stood in the middle of the intersection chatting like old buddies until the station wagon owner hurried over to a free-standing phone booth. The cops turned in unison and moved towards Will. The older cop, barrel-chested, with slits for eyes, spit out a toothpick before he swaggered over to the mashed grille of their Buick.

"Which one of you boys owns this vehicle?" he asked, the slit eyes facing the ex-hippie who stood outside the driver's door. Will wondered if the pale gold sheriff's badge pinned to the big man was genuine brass or just a piece of painted tin.

"I'm the driver," the ex-hippie said.

Will wiped away the new blood that trickled out of his nose. He listened to the ex-hippie launch into one of his non-stop, rambling narratives. He explained how the car belonged to his stepmother, how the insurance had run out and he was supposed to get new insurance but that she had forgotten to give him the title, which was where he was headed when the accident happened with the station wagon pulling in front of him. He was on his way home to Illinois to get the title. He knew it was illegal but he was sure they would understand, being as how they were fair, understanding men.

The big cop nodded then looked at Will. But it was the younger cop—skinny, with a pale, pimpled face that could have been mistaken for a teenager—who spoke.

"Who's the kid?"

"He's a drifter. I was giving him a ride."

"I'm no goddamned drifter," Will said, indignant. "I was hitchhiking."

"Let me see your license," the big cop ordered, turning back to the ex-hippie. After he glanced at the card the ex-hippie had pulled out of his back pocket, the sheriff nodded with a formal, bored air as if reading the license had made him tired.

"Well, your friend here can do as he pleases," the sheriff said. "But you're takin' a little ride with us."

On cue, the pimpled cop marched around the grill to lead the ex-hippie to the patrol car. The sheriff slipped the license into his front shirt pocket.

"What about me?" Will asked, amazed that they were going to just leave, let him fend for himself despite the fact that they could see he was bleeding, that he could even have a concussion. Will's mother was a nurse and he'd learned enough about medicine from her to know it was a possibility.

"How about ambulances?" Will added, angry that he had to ask for what should have been routine.

"We can call you one, son," the sheriff answered, the slits suddenly opening enough to show the whites of his eyes. "But you got to pay for it."

"Pay?" Will asked. He'd never heard of such a thing.

"On the spot," the sheriff said. "How much is a mo-bile unit, Trey?"

"'Bout fifty dollars," the pimpled cop answered, leading the ex-hippie to the patrol car.

"You want us to call you one?" the sheriff asked.

"If you don't mind walking," the young cop called from the patrol car. "The hospital be just up the road a piece."

The sheriff studied the mashed grill of the Buick, waiting for an answer.

"I don't have fifty bucks," Will said, wondering why the cops couldn't just drop him off. But he didn't ask.

"Alright, son," the sheriff said. "It ain't far. You'll get there before you know it."

It was dark by the time Will reached the small, municipal hospital. There were no sidewalks so he had to walk on the gravel shoulder of the boulevard, where the passing motorists sometimes tossed their cigarette butts, flying out of the open windows like sparks. He tried to take some comfort in the gold and crimson sky, a bigger sunset than anything he would ever see back home. But Will kept picturing the patrol car driving away, blue lights flashing, the ex-hippie, the acid freak who had almost got them killed, being chauffeured to safety while he, William Michaels—son of a prominent Maryland attorney, honors graduate of Haverford College, the only person actually *hurt* in the accident—was left to his own devices like some illegal migrant worker.

"You're smart to do this," the pretty slim nurse said as if, like the cops, there were some question about whether or not it was worth looking after his injury. Will noticed that he was the only person in the emergency room.

"People have died from these little concussions," she continued, her voice soft, appealing. "Why there was a man I knew who made the mistake of going to sleep after getting a bump on the head at a softball game and never did wake up again. Went right into a coma. He should have known better."

Will remained silent, enjoying the soft drawl of her voice and the smell of whatever sweet soap she bathed with. She kept a light, almost musical banter as she took him through a series of reflex tests. The last was tapping his knee caps with a small hammer to make his shin jerk.

"Well," she said, smiling at him, her blue eyes lit with a kind of impersonal, professional affection. "It looks like you'll be just fine. Your head is gonna ache for awhile but, by tomorrow, you'll be good as new. I'll slip you some aspirin in the meantime."

"I don't need it," Will said, standing up.

"You sure? Why don't you just take it with you? Wait just a minute."

The nurse, her figure hidden underneath the loose, formless whites, hurried to an office behind the counter. She returned with a clump of aspirin packages in her small hands.

"If anything gets worse," she said. "You just come right back here, alright?"

Will noticed her lipstick, caked on the way someone from her mother's generation might have worn it. Her face, too, was smooth with creams and blushes. He guessed it was just the way women in these small Texas towns wore make-up because the nurse certainly didn't need it.

"Can you tell me how to get to the bus station?" Will asked, having decided earlier that he would take a bus the rest of the way to New Orleans. The accident had made him more anxious than ever to keep moving, keep traveling. He feared stopping, settling in, the way other people feared change.

After the nurse had given him directions, they walked together toward the glass exit doors, past an old security guard who smiled at them like they were two kids on a date.

"Thanks for your help," Will said, preparing to leave. "I never got your name."

"Patricia," the nurse said, hesitating with him by the door. "My friends call me Trish."

"I've always liked that name," Will answered. "It's pretty. Like you."

The nurse smiled and glanced away, seeming half her age.

"It was nice meeting you," she said. "I think it's exciting what you're doing. Traveling around like you are. What an adventure. It's hard, you know, for a woman to do those things."

"It wouldn't be safe," Will agreed.

"Well, good luck," she said. "And you come straight back here if something feels bad. Promise?"

The glow of the streetlamps guided Will to the center of town. It was quiet except for the steady chortle of crickets. The pristine lawns and the subdued porch lights reminded him of his neighborhood, the one he had grown up in. It was safe there, comfortable the way this little town felt. There was much to be said for this life, he thought. He had been quick to dismiss it, to disdain the comfort and security, to feel he was somehow above it. But it felt good, there was no denying it. The only catch, he'd learned, was that it wasn't enough.

As Will turned the corner, he spotted a metal shingle hanging from a tall wood post in the middle of one of the manicured lawns. Moving closer and into the dim light of the post lamp, he read the metal sign: "Sheriff's Office/City Jail." The Sheriff's patrol car was parked in the white gravel lot behind the house, the stones shimmering like snow underneath the brilliant white haze of a spotlight. Will wondered if the ex-hippie was sitting in a jail cell, trying to talk his way out or calling his stepmother. Will decided to investigate. He still had plenty of time before his bus left.

The jail was in the basement. Will let himself in through the back screen door, feeling as if he was barging into a neighbor's kitchen at dinner, only instead of finding a family seated around an old wooden table, chattering, forks scraping their steaming plates, there was only the barrel-chested sheriff, stationed behind a metal desk, his pen scratching paper. He didn't look up until after the screen door clapped shut. He glanced at Will as if people always entered without knocking.

"Find the hospital OK?" the sheriff asked. Will noticed there were cool gray eyes where the dark slits used to be. The sheriff's manner was different, too. He was more polite, more attentive, like the cops that were friends of his father. Will suddenly dropped his resentment, his anger at having been forced to walk to the hospital. The cops hadn't meant anything personal. It was just the way things were done in Orange.

"Your friend's over there," the sheriff said pointing to the far corner of the room. The ex-hippie was sitting in the corner cell, staring at the floor.

"How long's he in for?"

"Don't know, son. He claims his stepmother is sending bail money from Michigan. We'll see."

"That could be days."

The sheriff hesitated, appraising Will, before he returned his attention to the papers on his desk.

"How much is bail?" Will asked.

"Fifteen dollars," the sheriff answered without looking up.

"Fifteen bucks?" Will said. "That's it?"

A short time later, Will and the ex-hippie were walking through the quiet neighborhood together on their way out of town. The ex-hippie introduced himself as David as they hurried along the sidewalk, thanking Will, swearing he'd pay the money back just as soon as he got to Michigan, to his stepmother's place. He wanted to know where Will was from, where he was going, what brought him to be traveling around the way he was; all the questions that had not been asked during their ride along the Gulf Coast.

Will was relieved when they came to the end of the quiet street and saw the green sign that showed the way to the Interstate entrance. David was hitchhiking his way back north and Will was anxious to get to the bus station. They shook hands, David repeating his promise to send money. Will watched the lone ex-hippie cross the dark street, then hurry up the expressway ramp, holding his thumb high in the air as he jogged toward the busy highway where red taillights streaked by like comets in the night sky.

Will saw a drifter suddenly, running to the edge of approach ramps, wandering from city to city, wherever the driver happened to be going. Although it had only been days since he'd been on those windy highways, it already felt like a distant memory. As the ex-hippie disappeared from view, absorbed by the dark road, Will found himself waving, hoping the drifter would find his way home.

The bus depot was a short stroll away. The station doubled as a general store, so Will bought himself a bag of salted pecans and a pint of milk for the ride to New Orleans. The bus was a bright red and silver Trailways with modern, airline-style seats that were familiar, reminding Will of vacations, of trips home from college. There were only a few passengers in the cavernous bus and most were sleeping. But it felt comforting to have people around, resting quietly.

As the big, heavy bus lumbered onto the narrow street, Will relaxed into his plush seat, closed his eyes as they drove out of Orange and immediately began musing about New Orleans, the famous French Quarter, thrilled by its promise of excitement, of an entirely different way of life from the one he knew. Somewhere in the midst of his imaginings, he fell asleep, a deep, dreamless sleep. So he didn't see the Buick as the bus rumbled by the garage, didn't see the mashed grill tilted high in the air, hoisted on a line that reeled from the pick-up truck's tow bar. It hung limply, dangling like the day's catch.

VIDEO VERITÉ & OTHER STORIES

WILLIAM PETRICK

Car Crazy

The last thing I wanted to do was sell the old Beemer. It had been my first purchase since the divorce, a time when I was having trouble caring about much of anything. But the car added a new dimension to my life, despite or maybe because of all the problems surrounding it. Like a love affair, the difficulties only fueled and intensified the passion. It was exhilarating to climb into the black leather cockpit, snap myself snugly into place with the cross belt, then ignite the fuel injectors and feel the sports car rumble to life. The controls on the German dashboard glowed amber, their abstract markings like some high tech hieroglyphics. In first gear, the coupe shot from its docking space, hurled down West End Avenue like it was being fired into the autobahn. My own pulse raced as it flew under yellow traffic lights, past timid clunkers that I spotted shaking to a halt in my rear view mirror.

The man that wanted to buy the car was a former minister who revered the car. For weeks this kind, spiritual shepherd tried to talk me out of selling it. He somberly assured me that times would certainly improve one day and then I would regret selling it to him. He urged me to reconsider. I took two weeks, worried that the sudden appearance of a minister, a messenger of God, was an omen.

There had been other strangers suddenly appearing to save the car. The first had materialized on an empty stretch of highway outside Harlem. I was driving home from a poetry reading one cold night in early April, exactly a week after I'd purchased the car, when the lights and radio cut off without warning, the once powerful, speeding coupe drifted to a dead stop in the middle of the highway. It was well after midnight and there were few cars on the dark road. One of the busted streetlamps buzzed and sputtered. I tried pushing the car. I remember thinking I probably looked like some scared white yuppie, at least to people who lived in a place like Harlem. The irony was that I didn't fit into the world of privilege, either.

When the car wouldn't budge, I tried flagging down a good Samaritan. To my surprise, the first car stopped. The driver backed up, lined his old clunker behind my moribund car and pushed me to an all-night gas station on 96th Street. We never spoke. He kept his dark window sealed shut and rumbled away wordlessly as I steered into the Mobil station.

But this time around, it was my rising debt, not another spirit that appeared before me and I had to call the minister back. The afternoon he was to pick it up, I hurried home from my temp job to empty my things out of the glove compartment and the small trunk. There wasn't much in the glove compartment: a couple of old spark plugs, a clump of old parking tickets. The trunk had a pair of stiff, dried out boat shoes, a half-empty can of car wax, a greasy rag for checking the oil and a damp beach towel. As I rolled everything into the towel, planning to throw the bundle out, I spotted Scott's tools. The sight of them filled me with an instant, wistful melancholy like stumbling upon an old photograph of a childhood friend. The tools were lying in a corner, exactly as my mechanic had left them. It was typical of him. He was absent-minded, the way brilliant, talented professors can be.

Scott was a gifted mechanic. He made precise engine adjustments by ear and feel when others had to rely on the latest digital electronics. His accuracy was uncanny. I'd watch him operate, fascinated by his surgical skill and his obvious passion for performing it. My house mates, all young, successful New Yorkers, found it amusing that I'd act as an apprentice to a shy recluse who looked more like a homeless person in need of a bath and shave than a qualified mechanic. But I wanted to learn about cars and engine design the way others might yearn to know more about history or astronomy. I would hand Scott a question with each tool, wanting to know exactly what he was doing and why.

"Your friend is on the phone," Sabrina would tease, giving me a sly, coquettish smile as she slipped the receiver into my hand.

"He's got a crush on you," I'd answer, smiling back. I liked her too. She knew it the way she knew we could be friends.

"Hmm," she purred, staying so close that I could smell the expensive perfume that oozed from her slim neck.

Sabrina was the house socialite, a dark-eyed, Serbian beauty who seemed to know where and when every party was taking place in the Hamptons. Most telephone calls, in fact, were about parties or day after reports about parties. Most of these bashes were held at the homes of the wealthy, the kind with swimming pools and tennis courts. No one ever seemed to know the host or worried about knowing the host. There was music, free drinks, and hundreds of strangers. I was uncomfortable at these anonymous parties but I went anyway, each time hoping I'd feel more at ease, more a part of what was going on.

Scott couldn't have been more out of place. He was thin, nervous, with a balding head that he hid with a soiled navy blue baseball cap. It was rare to find his long face unblemished with the grime of the garage. His clothes, too, were threadbare and woven with the grease and soot of cars. But he didn't care about his appearance. He cared about cars. He needed to repair automobiles the way born painters needed to paint or musicians needed to play. Scott made a living off of his skill but most of the money went to child support or, as I later discovered, was never collected in the first place. He was not a money manager.

This indifference to money was fortunate for me. Maintaining a luxury car, even one as old as mine, was very expensive, a detail I'd managed to overlook in my fervor to own it, to start a new, better life. There was always some small, annoying problem. But Scott would always appear like a mystical guardian. When it came time to pay, he'd insist on collecting only what I could afford.

"You'll make it up when you're back in the high life," he said once when I could only afford twenty dollars for an engine adjustment that would have cost hundreds at a garage. "When I get my own shop, I'm gonna need investors. Then I'll come looking for you."

Scott's chances of owning and running his private repair garage were slight, despite his enormous talent. He would need big time investors, real estate and above all, a staff he would have to manage. All were beyond his reach even though I liked to fantasize along with him. I liked to picture Scott with his own shop, working on cars, educating a class of young, eager mechanics. But Scott worked solo and he had a troublesome past that few investors would ignore. Still, I never stopped hoping to be proved wrong.

The payback, however, came sooner than expected and in a form that neither of us could have imagined. It happened one gray morning in February, when the icy wind off the Hudson was so brittle that it made my eyes tear just running out to buy the newspaper. Scott called, insisting on delivering my car to Manhattan. As usual, he had made repairs worth hundreds, maybe thousands, charged me next to nothing and now was volunteering to deliver the car. It was an extraordinary gesture, even for Scott. I glanced out my studio window at the steel grey sky, heard the angry whine of that winter wind and imagined what it would feel like walking to the subway station.

"What time can you be here?" I asked.

A few hours later, he was climbing up the old, wood stairs of my fifth story walk-up. My wife had stayed in our two bedroom apartment, along with all the better furniture. I should have negotiated for at least a few good pieces. But I was desperate to get out, to escape the strained civility that we had adopted when speaking to one another. I couldn't bear sleeping on the stiff futon mattress on the floor of the spare room that we had once planned for a child.

Scott stumbled into my tiny studio, glancing at the low ceiling as if concerned about its' safety then collapsed into a table chair near the window. He slouched, gripping his right thigh.

"Nice place," he lied.

"What's wrong with your leg?"

"It's been swelling up. The fucker aches, so I been tryin' to stay off it."

"Anybody look at it?"

"What for? One of these doctors is gonna look at it, tell me it's swollen, then charge me a hundred bucks for telling me what I already know."

"Maybe it's serious."

"It ain't serious. It just aches. What I got to do is stay off it."

Scott had no health insurance so I could understand his reluctance to see a doctor. But his bad leg made me wonder why he insisted on delivering the car when he was in no condition to do it. As if guessing my thoughts, Scott sat up.

"I need a favor," he said. He wanted me to drive him by an apartment building in Washington Heights because he wanted to give money to a single Hispanic mother who he'd promised to look after.

"I told Rosita I'd look after her and her girl. I give them a little money."

"Rosita?" I'd never heard him mention her before.

"I fixed her car. She broke down on the Cross Bronx and I was driving by. I figured what the shit. Can't just leave the woman."

"This isn't about picking up some coke is it?" I asked.

"I told you. I'm off that shit," Scott answered. "I've learned my lesson. I got divorce and bankruptcy to prove it."

Sitting in my apartment, eyes roving the room, he did seem more jittery than usual. But then there was his leg. It was obvious he was in pain. Despite the injury, he'd delivered the car to my doorstep. The least I could do was make the short drive up to Washington Heights. I'd be up and back in less than half an hour. Besides, it would be fun to race up the West Side Highway.

As we drove to the Heights, his soiled hands dug into the seat as he tried to joke about not getting laid since he was married.

"I ain't got all these city babes like you. Mine's gonna fall off soon like an old rusted tail pipe," he said with a pained smile. I remembered the crush he'd had on Sabrina, saw his instant shyness when she smiled her sexy, flirtatious smile. I'd introduced them when Sabrina complained of having engine trouble with her Italian convertible. A week later, Scott handed me a new oil filter.

"This is for Sabrina," he said, then pretended to look for a wrench in his tool box.

"Anything you want me to say?"

"Just give it to her."

The Washington Heights neighborhood was dismal. Middle-aged men, mostly black and Hispanic, loitered outside a run-down bodega. Trashed drifted down the sidewalk. There was a bleak, cold hostility lingering behind the old, uncared for buildings. Scott hobbled into the projects while I double-parked. It was the kind of slum where drugs flourished. But I didn't care if Scott was conning me. I was paying back a favor. I just hoped we were gone before a blue and white NYPD sedan cruised by.

I was relieved when Scott finally stumbled back out of the cement building, his clothes flapping from his skinny, awkward body like a walking scarecrow.

After he'd pulled himself back inside, he asked me to drop him off at the train station so that he could get back to his rented room on Long Island. As I hurried us out of the neighborhood, however, it became obvious he was in severe pain, aggravated by the visit to Rosita.

"How was Rosita?"

"She was OK," he said, clenching his teeth.

"Why don't I drop you off at the hospital."

"I told you. I ain't going to a doctor."

We turned onto the main boulevard and I down-shifted, enjoying the smooth, silky gearing. Scott hadn't just repaired the clutch. He'd improved it. Only new cars shifted this smoothly.

"I'm not just going to leave you off at the train station. You can barely walk."

"I'll be OK. Thanks."

We stopped at a red light. Ahead was the entrance to the George Washington Bridge which led to New Jersey. To the left was the entrance to the West Side Highway that would take us back to the city.

"What about your family. Aren't they in New Jersey?"

Scott was silent. I didn't have the time to drive him all the way to New Jersey but I also wasn't comfortable leaving him to fend for himself at the train station.

"My old man has a shop in Tenafly," he said and his face brightened. "He might be able to help out."

"How far a drive is that?"

"Forty minutes."

It was my turn to be silent. My short trip was turning into a two-hour journey. I wanted to help but not that much.

"Just take me to the train station," Scott said, staring at the green light. I should have been relieved. Instead, I felt even more responsible.

"You won't even make it down the escalator," I said and shot under the light towards the entrance to the George Washington.

As we sped across the bridge, past the soaring web of cables, Scott warned me that his old man was unlikely to welcome him with open arms.

"He thinks I'm a fuck-up," Scott said. He paused, gazing out at the bare, imposing cliffs of the Palisades. I thought to tell him once about the disappointment that colored my father's once proud eyes, how he would suddenly muse over the possibilities of what his son might have become. He viewed my broken marriage, my dying business as irrevocable failures, the sign of a man who just couldn't get his life together. Sometimes, I was afraid he might be right.

Scott's father was a ruddy-faced, corpulent business man. He eyed me with suspicion, a flicker of dislike in his glance. Scott attempted to explain his leg injury but as soon as he began, his father's eyes darkened and a cool indifference spread across his wide, well-fed face. Scott might have hit on his father for help before, then threw it away on drugs. Still, his father's refusal to help infuriated me. I'd been raised to believe that you stood by your family no matter what. When I started to speak, intending to remind Scott's father of his responsibility, Scott waved me to silence and limped back inside the car. He apologized for dragging me to the middle of New Jersey and asked to be dropped off at the train station.

"I can't just leave you like this," I said, even though that was exactly what I wanted. This whole trip was getting out of hand. I couldn't afford to miss the four o'clock meeting with my client. It was an important account, my only account. I had to be there. There was no one to cover for me. My partner had left the business years earlier and I had worked alone, as a free lancer, ever since.

"You got work. It's OK."

I stopped at the red light and watched the passing traffic on the boulevard. The dead grass marooned on the median strip was the color of straw and the car fumes swirled over it like cigarette smoke. Across the boulevard was a strip parking lot and an electrical supply company housed in drab cement block. It was the battered, industrial part of New Jersey that I loathed and it made me anxious to get back home.

"You can turn right on red," Scott said, his eyes fastened on the traffic light. There was a distance in his voice, a sense of resignation. But he was neither angry nor sorry for himself. It was, as he often said about his struggles, just the way things were. I admired his ability to accept whatever was thrown at him.

We drove along the boulevard in silence. The mid-afternoon sun was a pale winter white but its glare forced me to squint. I regretted leaving my sunglasses on the desk in my studio. But of course I'd assumed the ride to Washington Heights would be brief. I should have known better. I should have known about getting involved with Scott. Now I was on this pathetic road in the middle of the day, driving around with a guy nobody wanted.

"You mind stopping by a phone?" Scott asked. He was hunched over, holding his leg. The side of his face looked as pale as the winter sun.

"Who you going to call?"

"My wife. My ex-wife."

Scott opened the door and lifted his leg with his hands and set it outside the car as if it was a piece of board. He used the roof and door well to pull the rest of his body out. How was he going to get himself down the cement stairs at Penn Station, through the rush hour crowds and find a seat on a train jammed with commuters desperate to get home to their families? How was he going to get to his rented room if he did make it to the train station at the other end? He never talked about having any friends.

Scott's phone call was brief. In less than a minute, he was loading himself back into the car. I didn't have to ask what his ex-wife's response had been. It was clear in his ashen face. He was alone.

"Where's the closest hospital?" I asked.

"Don't know."

"Yeah, you do. Cut the shit, Scott. I'm not dropping you off at any train station until we go to a hospital. Got it? You need help."

The car accelerated down the boulevard like it was on a test track. I started passing cars, weaving from lane to lane, using the speed and dexterity of the sports sedan. We didn't need a flashing red light.

"They'll give you tickets out here," Scott warned, sitting up straight for the first time. He smiled, proud of the car's performance.

The Emergency Room was a caricature of itself. A snide, bored old woman, sat smugly behind the Plexiglas, insisting that Scott answer each procedural question. By now, Scott's eyes were watering from the pain and he was twisting in his wheelchair, struggling not to scream. Still, the grey haired woman returned a look of insufferable boredom and asked his age, date of birth, occupation. It didn't occur to her that this was a procedure that could wait until he was at least relieved of his pain.

"Hey, lady," I said, stepping in front of Scott. "Can't you see the guy is in pain? Are you blind?"

The gray hair stared back at me with her blank fish eyes.

"We are required to follow procedures."

I stopped a young, blonde nurse who happened to be walking through the waiting room. She was friendly and eager to help and there was a clear, untroubled confidence in her blue eyes that reminded me of people I'd known in college, people I'd been surrounded with my entire life. A few minutes later, she opened the door as I wheeled Scott into the emergency room.

No medical staff made an appearance for half an hour. Scott was dumb with pain. He could not speak. He could only cling to his pain. He was beyond stoicism. Frustrated, I wandered into the ER records area and found a doctor, asking if they'd forgotten about my friend. They had. A few minutes later, an Asian doctor appeared and examined Scott's bulging leg.

"You're a friend?"

For a long, silent moment, I simply stared at the doctor. The question had never occurred to me. He was my mechanic. Finally, I nodded, startled into recognition. I was his friend. I cared about him, not just what he could do for me.

"It's a good thing you made it here when you did," the doctor said.

"Why is that?"

"He's got a blood clot in his leg. It could have traveled up to his heart and cut off all circulation. Might have killed him."

Scott was momentarily lucid before they wheeled him to the operating room, relieved by the promise of treatment. He made one request, the only serious request he'd made since the ordeal began. He asked me to call his father. He would need a ride home when he woke up from the operation.

"I'll wait," I said.

"You done enough. Just call him."

"I can drive back."

Scott shook his head, his lips pressed tight. I'd offended him. He didn't want anyone feeling sorry for him. He clung to his last bit of pride as the gurney squeaked down the white tile floor.

"Your son is in the operating room," I said, contemptuous of Scott's father even though I had never met him. "He's going to need someone to pick him up."

There was a startled silence. I was glad to hear it.

"What happened now?" his father asked. I told him about the blood clot. Again, there was the silence, the calculation.

"What time do I need to come?" his father asked. It was my turn to be surprised. For a few moments, I couldn't speak. It was as if my own father had suddenly had a change of heart.

"A few hours," I said, finally. "He'll call you."

"OK."

"You'll come get him, right?" I asked, suspicious.

"Yes. Of course I will."

The car drove for nearly a year without developing a single problem. I checked up on Scott once during that time, a short telephone conversation with his father. Soon after his release from the hospital, he'd gone to work fixing cars at the family business.

"He's one hell of a mechanic," his father said.

"Best I've ever seen."

My own fortunes rebounded and I was able to move out of the tiny studio with the claustrophobic ceilings. For the first time since my marriage ended, I felt like I had a home. At the same time, being in a relationship began to look attractive again. In many ways, I was emerging from my shell of disappointments, ready to stick my head out in the risky air. As spring approached, however, there were signs that my success was faltering once again. The New York *Times* called the city's sudden breakdown an "economic downturn." My friends called it a recession.

As if on cue, the car broke down. Scott's father tersely announced a new telephone number for his son. As always, Scott responded immediately but asked me to drive the car to a repair shop in Upper Nyack, an affluent Hudson River town. He didn't say anything about his father's business or why he wasn't working there anymore.

Moments after I arrived, an angry customer pounced on Scott, demanding that his car be repaired immediately. He'd paid Scott for the job and it wasn't finished. The man's anger made his pale, jowly face even uglier. It made me think of a bull dog with saliva lapping from its mouth.

I learned later that this customer had paid less than five hundred dollars for a job that would have cost thousands anywhere else. Scott, in his absent-minded professor way, had been poking along on the job as he tried to juggle other repairs. This bull dog, however, wanted his deal. He knew, as I did, that Scott would do great work. He also shrewdly surmised that Scott would do quality work for little money. That's all the man knew or wanted to know. When Scott apologized and promised he'd finish it within the week, the man went livid, insisting a deal was a deal. His flushed face bulged through the car window.

"So how did you end up here?" I asked, handing him a wrench as he worked on an old Mercedes.

"I grew up in Nyack. About two blocks from here."

"This is a nice neighborhood."

"Used to be. So what's wrong with the car?"

After I'd given him my diagnosis, I told him about the economic downturn. It was severe enough that I might have to sell the car. Scott stopped working when he heard this, but I couldn't see his face. It was blocked by the open hood of the car.

"I might be able to get you an old clunker," he said, after a long pause. "At least it'll get you around."

"I can't afford anything. I'm back to trains and buses from here on out. No more cars."

Before leaving that night, I watched him play outside with his dog in the white, hazy light of the garage. I sensed that this would be the last time I would see Scott. The car had brought our lives together and its maintenance had kept the friendship running. But that would soon be over. The car would have a new guardian.

I wondered what would come of Scott. He now kept his clothes and whatever other valuables he owned in the trunk of the old LeSabre that he kept running when every other mechanic had given it up to the garbage heap. The dog, I knew, was his only companion. I knew, too, that he would stay up all night to try and catch up on his work and not succeed. Another bull dog would breathe down his back, demanding that he make good on his deal. Scott would not even have time to take a shower.

The minister was due any minute. I hurried to clean the windows. I wanted my car to shine. But after spraying the front window shield with the blue cleaner, I became aware of being watched. I looked across the street but there was nothing but parked cars and the brick wall of a school. But when I checked above the wall at the fence that protected the playground, there were two cherubic school girls, gazing down at me. They seemed to have appeared out of thin air. They watched patiently as I continued to clean the windows. The girls were animated with innocent interest and I could feel that they were enjoying themselves. I waved to them. This made them shy and they pawed the fence.

"Is that your car?" the little blonde angel asked suddenly.

"Not for long," I said, blocking the rust-colored sun with one hand so I could get a better look at the schoolgirls.

"That's a really great car," she said and then they vanished.

The wire fence continued to shake after they disappeared. There were faint, distant shrieks of kids at play. The growing traffic rumbled in the background. The approaching dusk had softened the light to a burnished gold with streaks of tangerine painted in the blue sky behind the spires of the Gothic church that towered at the end of the block.

The polished flank of the car gleamed in the fading light like a sleek, gray shark. The headlights peered arrogantly from either side of the sloping hood. There were gill-like slits to allow air to flow to the powerful engine. Even at rest, the car gave the illusion of movement, of great speed, of unspeakable grace. I'd never before had such pride in ownership. I wondered if caretakers of great art had this feeling when they looked upon the timeless paintings entrusted to their walls. Someone had taken great care and skill to craft this car and, if it wasn't exactly art, it was or had become a kind of sublime creation for me. It was also largely Scott's creation, the living proof of a gifted mechanic who treasured his craft.

I tried to call him after that night in the old colonial town. I'd promised to give him more money when the car was sold. Scott didn't care, insisting there was no need to worry about him. He'd collect after I was back in the high life. But when I called the Nyack garage, the chief mechanic told me that Scott had left town. There was an impatience in his voice that made me suspect Scott might have been fired.

"Do you know where?"

"No. Scott just goes wherever he feels like it," the man answered.

All the other phone numbers Scott once gave me turned up nothing. Even his father's home number rung up only a ghost. A recording informed me that the number had been disconnected. There was no new number.

"Sorry I'm late," the minister said, strolling up the sidewalk. He stopped, admiring his new car. There was a look of pride in his eyes, a kind of happy disbelief at his own good fortune that suddenly put me at ease.

"Gave me a chance to clean it up," I said.

"You don't need to do that," he said, smiling. "Believe me, my son will have this polished like a trophy."

"Do you have a mechanic?" I asked. "It needs a good mechanic. Somebody that really knows what he's doing," I warned.

"Don't worry," the minister said, putting his hand on my shoulder.

I still think about Scott every time I see an old Beemer speed past. They're joined together in my mind. I can't see one of those gemlike cars without seeing that brilliant mechanic. I'm reminded of his rare talent, his painstaking care, his almost spiritual devotion to his craft. But, most of all, I see us driving together to that hospital, feeling the drab midday traffic slip behind us, sensing the unspeakable grace of a car in flawless form, called to save two lives in the balance.

Crossing Water

It's not until the train bursts out from behind the trees and onto the low iron trestles, so low as to be skimming over open water, that Eddie finally relaxes. The tenseness in his broad shoulders, the thick neck that strains under the barrage of city noise and crowds and restless energy, sinks into the foam backrest. He's anticipated this precious solitude from the moment he waved good-bye to Maria.

A few sailboats are moored along a distant, hazy shore, their silver masts as still as the river. Eddie feels a special link to the water, to the river shores of Maryland, even though he grew up in the suburbs of Baltimore without a dock in sight. He wonders if this kinship with water has anything to do with E.W., who has always wanted to live alongside a river. It's one of the few dreams his father has ever ventured to share.

E.W. has always been reluctant to reveal his feelings so it alarmed but did not surprise Eddie when he learned that E.W. had collapsed the day before without warning, his body overcome with the exhaustion of his silent, stoic fight against pneumonia. It was why neither weeks of cold sweats in the middle of hot, muggy nights, nor coughing fits and pearls of phlegm inspired even so much as a complaint. E.W. endured, steeling himself against anything or anyone that would try to get the best of him.

The train plunges back into a new corridor of trees. Eddie waits, almost holding his breath, knowing that there is one more bridge left, one more chance to glimpse the tranquil bay before even the trees disappear and the train lumbers past the old brick row houses and the marble steps of East Baltimore and the green, oxidized dome marking the center of Johns Hopkins Hospital.

Eddie wants to have his father transferred to the choice spot near the room's only window but E.W. isn't interested in a view of the lush trees or the sky changing colors at sunset.

"I can see it from here," his father says. Eddie knows that his father prefers the hospital TV dangling from the low ceiling.

"You just missed your mother," E.W. says.

"We talked," Eddie answers. In fact, he and his mother arranged to take turns being with E.W. so that he would not have to spend time alone.

"Would you please hand me that comb?" E.W. asks, motioning behind him like he's thumbing a ride. It surprises Eddie since his father so rarely asks for assistance. But he can see that it's difficult for E.W. to move. There's an oxygen tube clipped to the end of his long nose and a plastic IV taped to his thin, pale forearm.

His father sits up, finally, and bows his narrow head as if he's about to receive a benediction. He combs out his fine, white hair until the eyes and broad forehead are nearly hidden. The intelligent blue eyes burn through the white veil with an intensity that only comes with a fever.

"Just because I'm in a hospital bed doesn't mean I can't maintain a little dignity," his father says, bristling with annoyance. There are things men fear more than death, Eddie thinks. Plato said it was honor. For E.W., it's looking sloppy.

E.W. makes a part on one side, revealing darker roots that have resisted aging, then carefully slides the plastic comb across the crown of his head, smooths his hair until it's flat and neat. Eddie admires his father's intense concentration, the way he has always performed even the most simple acts with a Zenlike focus. He can picture his father bent over the kitchen counter, silently carving roast beef for a holiday meal with the gravity of prayer.

"The car still running hot?" his father asks suddenly. Eddie doesn't answer. He isn't sure what to talk about but it's not cars.

"What happened?" his father asks.

"Nothing," Eddie says. "It still overheats."

Eddie can feel the judgment underneath his father's stern blue gaze, an anger quivering below the surface. He knows that E.W. would like him to take better care of his car, to demonstrate what his father calls "pride of ownership."

"Yeah. I've tried everything," Eddie continues, feeling a need to defend himself although he hasn't done anything wrong. "Had the radiator flushed, the thermostat replaced, the hoses. But it still jumps up into the red when I get stuck in traffic."

E.W.'s long, brooding face absorbs the information. E.W. is prone to somber moods, although Eddie knows his father would never admit to having them. In his own mind, he has never been depressed, never succumbed to despair. It would be a sign of weakness.

"It's an old car," E.W. says finally. "It sounds like the head gasket is ready to go."

Eddie nods too, pretending he knows what a head gasket is.

"It's a metal ring that controls oil pressure in the engine," E.W. explains, a trace of amusement on his lips. "They can last as many as 200,000 miles. But when they go, you're out of an engine."

"So maybe I'll get the gasket replaced."

"The engine has to be completely taken apart, then put back together. Piece by piece. You're paying him by the hour, don't forget. It's more than you want to spend."

"How do you know how much I want to spend?" Eddie thinks of saying but doesn't. The authority and confidence of his father's voice muffles his own.

"It's not worth it for a car that old," his father continues. "You'd be better off buying a new one."

"I don't like new cars," Eddie answers. "They all look the same, drive the same, smell the same. I like the old ones. Something with a little history."

"History, young man," E.W. says, "demands a little maintenance."

Their conversation is interrupted by a new patient. He's wheeled into the choice spot under the window and Eddie is immediately resentful. His father should have the best location whether he wants it or not. But now it's too late.

The square of sky is now streaked with rose, the tops of the lush trees are a deep, summer green. He imagines opening the window and flooding the cool, de-odorized room with the heavy August air, sweet with the smell of grass and the chittering of cicadas. But it's against hospital policy and Eddie knows that E.W. prefers the air-conditioning anyway.

The new patient is in his fifties, much younger than his father, with plump, ruddy cheeks and a lively but gentle demeanor. He seems personable with the kind of easy, un-adult enthusiasm that Eddie associates with good teachers.

"You've got a roommate, E.W.," Eddie says, pleased that his father will have company. Eddie considers striking up a conversation but he hesitates, knowing it will make his father uncomfortable.

There is a young couple standing at the foot of the bed. The pretty, dark-haired woman is resting her hand on his ankle, smiling as she speaks. Eddie admires the ease of her gesture, touching her father without fear or self-consciousness. The husband stands alongside her, mute and respectful. A soldier.

"It was inevitable," E.W. says, disappointed that he will no longer have the room to himself.

Eddie hesitates calling Maria before he goes to sleep. He's worn out and doesn't want to talk, to answer the questions he knows his girlfriend will ask. But he also knows she'll wait up, anxious to hear the news. If he doesn't call, if he just takes some more time for himself, she won't understand. She'll accuse him of holding back, of being afraid to share his feelings.

As he raises the antenna of the cordless phone, Eddie pictures Maria on their couch, snuggled in the afghan, her thick glasses glowing with blue TV light. She only wears her glasses late at night when no one except Eddie is around to catch her in them.

"How is he?" she asks. The eagerness in her voice reminds Eddie of how deeply Maria worries when anyone in her family is sick with even a cold.

"He's as pale as a corpse," Eddie answers, then hesitates, needing to push away the fear. "But I think he's going to be OK. He's a tough old man. And they haven't found any cancer yet."

Maria is quiet, listening closely, more closely than Eddie wants her to listen.

"How are you?"

"Me?" Eddie says as though the question is beside the point. "I'm fine."

"You don't sound fine."

"I'm fine," Eddie insists but his voice doesn't even feel like his own.

"You can be afraid and angry and upset, you know. Your father is very sick. You're allowed," Maria says.

Eddie says nothing. Her anxious insistence makes him regret making the phone call.

"I hate when you do this," Maria continues. Her voice takes on a critical, arrogant tone, scolding like an overbearing mother. "You pretend like you're not feeling anything. Make yourself think that everything is just fine, fine, fine. It drives me crazy."

"It's a hard time," Eddie manages to say, wishing she would accept that he was tired, accept that at this moment, it frightened him to talk about his father dying.

"OK," she answers, flippantly. He can picture her throwing up her hands as if to say 'I tried, I tried.'

"I'll call you tomorrow," Eddie says.

Eddie stands by the telephone long after he has hung up. The conversation, like so many they have had before tonight, reminds him of the decision that needs to be made, has asked to be made for years, a choice that even moving in together did little to clarify for Eddie. He hoped that time would somehow tell him whether or not stay with Maria, as if future events would somehow make clear what he already knew, had known for longer than he cared to admit to himself.

The curtains flap in the heavy breeze like loose sails. When Eddie opens his eyes, in fact, he imagines he's glimpsing the morning sky over a white boat rail, not the windowsill of his old bedroom. He stares at the flutter of the curtains, smells the moist, morning air, tinged with brine. A breeze off the Chesapeake Bay. He remembers a time he'd gone sailing with E.W., one of the few trips they had ever taken together.

It was a hot, muggy afternoon and they'd dropped anchor in order to fix a line that had gotten tangled on a halyard. E.W. had been steering and had not responded to a sudden change in wind direction. He piloted according to the instructions in the sailing manual. Even when those instructions didn't work, which was often, he insisted on following the manual, certain that sooner or later the book would prove correct and the boat and the wind would do what they were supposed to do.

But as Eddie climbed up to fix the dangling line, his father suddenly took off his Oriole cap, boat shoes and white T-shirt and dove expertly into the pale gold water. There were sea nettles everywhere, floating by like lumps of murky Jell-o. E.W. was oblivious to the danger of being stung. He swam with measured, graceful strokes, utterly at peace in the water. When he climbed back on deck, there were none of the telltale red splotches on his lanky torso or his skinny legs, no sign that he had been touched by a single sea nettle.

"Good swim?" Eddie asked.

E.W. grinned, water dripping over his chiseled cheekbones and solid, square jaw. He seemed younger than his 64 years and, for a moment, Eddie glimpsed his father as the cocky adolescent that he claimed he had been.

"Did you see the sea nettles?" Eddie asked.

He shrugged. "They're always around this time of year."

Eddie had seen a neighbor who had been stung by sea nettles. A hot, red welt branded his back and he shivered from the pain, sweating like he had a fever.

"Water's warm," Dad said. "Try it."

Eddie was stung the moment he dove into the water. A sharp pain shot up his back like he'd been stabbed by a long needle. He was stung again in the arm as he raced back to the boat and pricked in the thigh as he clambered back on the deck, feeling nauseous from all the poison. E.W. stood alongside the rudder, watching with a distant curiosity.

"Vinegar takes away the sting," he said.

"Where the hell are we going to get vinegar in the middle of the bay?"

E.W. nodded, peering at the wounds.

"You should know better than to listen to me," he said.

They laughed, a short utterly spontaneous outburst that rippled across the tranquil bay, drifting into the pale marsh grass along the shore. His father's bright grin spread across his narrow face, a gold filling glinting from a back tooth, deep creases rising from the corner of his narrowed blue eyes. Eddie felt, in that unexpected moment, as though they were not father and son at all but two boys, playing together on the water in the middle of a hot and lazy summer afternoon.

The teacher has cancer. In less than twenty-four hours, this energetic man has gone from ruddy cheeks to ashen face, vacant eyes. E.W. says they wheeled him in before dawn and he's either been sleeping or staring at the ceiling. The swiftness of the change stuns Eddie and, like rubbernecking at an accident, he can't help himself from staring.

"They said the cancer has spread all through his lungs. It doesn't look good."

"You've talked to him?"

"No. I wouldn't put that burden on him."

"What burden?" Eddie asks.

"Don't shout," his father says.

"What burden are you talking about?"

Why, Eddie wants to ask, why are people always such a burden to you?

"He needs the people closest to him right now. Not strangers."

"Maybe he could use a friend, E.W."

"I'm not a friend."

"Never too late."

"It's more difficult when you're older. And when you're in a place like this. Imagine yourself in his situation. Would you want your family by your side or an old man who's as pale as you are?"

"You're not that pale," Eddie lies.

"Getting old is terrible," his father says as though he hasn't heard Eddie. "But he's a young man, still. Many years ahead of him and he has to endure this."

His father has always urged Eddie to take the time to examine a situation from the other person's point of view. It was part of his training and experience as a trial lawyer but E.W. also added an empathy that was as warm and natural as his impulse to remain private and distant. The contradiction had the effect of making Eddie inwardly protective of his father, of that fragile sensitivity secreted inside a stiff, hardened shell. Eddie wanted to coax him out, to engage his father. But E.W. was resentful of any prodding and would only expose himself for a moment and then only under his own impulse before he would sink back inside himself, stubbornly content to remain unknown, unseen.

The next day Eddie volunteers to wait with E.W. for his cancer test. His father is lying on his gurney just outside the operating room. They don't talk. E.W. is uncomfortable having his son waiting there with him. He doesn't like people helping him. He likes to do things alone.

"You don't have to wait," E.W. says. "There's nothing to be done."

"I don't mind," Eddie answers, trying to sound casual, afraid to reveal how important it is to be standing alongside his father. "I'm here. Might as well keep you company."

A doctor is paged in the corridor, the name made incoherent by the bright acoustics of the bare tile. The ward, however, is otherwise quiet as though the staff has left. A modern, electric clock hums faintly, the red second hand sweeps underneath the immobile black arms of the hours and minutes.

E.W. has collected clocks for years, especially wrist watches. Eddie, who doesn't wear a watch, thinks his father's interest in timepieces is eccentric. E.W.'s favorite watch is his own father's retirement gift, a wrist watch received shortly before his death. Eddie thinks it's an ugly watch, a plain face shrouded in murky glass, a reminder in many ways of Grandfather himself, a tired, aloof man whose disinterested bug eyes remained forever sheathed behind special glasses as thick as the bottom of old milk bottles. But Eddie couldn't mistake the pride glowing in E.W.'s face the day he first displayed the watch, passing it gingerly in his open palm like a collector with a priceless treasure and his father staring into the clouded glass as though it held some secret, wondering, perhaps, about his own father.

"So what actually happens in this test?" Eddie asks.

"They insert a long probe into your lungs, take a sample of the tissue, then withdraw it."

"Sounds painful."

"It's uncomfortable."

"They give you anesthetics, right?"

"If you chose."

"You'd have to be crazy not to chose them."

E.W. looks up at the ceiling, his mind already somewhere else, somewhere deep inside himself. But he seems to appreciate Eddie standing alongside, keeping him company. Eddie knows because his father looks at him as if he'd never seen Eddie before and says "You're a good son."

Eddie, who is uneasy with praise of any kind, is suddenly filled with gratitude. He thinks this is a good moment to tell his father how much he admires and loves him but E.W. is not looking at him. His eyes are downcast, introspective, and there is a deep disappointment in his gaze, a sense of loss.

"How long are they going to make you wait?"

"Look at these floors," E.W. says. The tile is old and could use a fresh coat of wax but it's clean. "If they treat their floors like that, how do you think they'll treat patients?"

"Different staff, E.W. Doctors and nurses don't clean the floors."

"Still the same management. If they took pride in this hospital they wouldn't let the floors get so run down."

"You want me to get you a mop?" Eddie asks.

"Hell no," his father answers but Eddie isn't so sure. E.W. loves to clean things, anything. Once, while in high school, Eddie had come home from his varsity baseball game and found E.W. in the driveway washing the car but with the hood up as if he were fixing the engine at the same time.

"How'd you do?" his father asked without looking up.

"Two hits, one RBI. But you didn't miss much. We lost by four," Eddie answered, watching his father diligently scrubbing his car engine.

"Well, you did your best," his father answered as he squinted into the white suds bubbling up from the black engine casing. "That's all you can do. Just do the best you can."

"Can I ask you something, Dad?"

"I'm listening."

"Why are you washing the engine?"

"Engines get dirty. Oil builds up."

"I've never heard of anyone washing their engine," Eddie said.

"That, young man, is because you're allergic to washing cars."

In the evening, Eddie sits in his father's oak swivel chair. The seat is polished smooth by wear. This is E.W.'s private room. His law books line the shelves, diplomas are displayed on the wall. There is a large photograph, too, of his father pleading a case before the Supreme Court. He appears cool and collected in his tailored gray suit, his unwavering gaze an emblem of integrity.

Inside the broad, executive desk, which no one has ever been allowed to explore, is everything that E.W. saves: from old WWII photographs to coin collections to insurance policies. Eddie knows about these only because he's made himself a nuisance in the past, making sure to accidentally barge into the den, hoping to catch his father off-guard.

Tonight, however, Eddie has the key. His mother has asked that he check to see that the papers are in order. Just in case the test comes back negative, which is what the doctors predict. So Eddie looks through many of the brown, legal files, burning with curiosity. Thirty years of secrecy yielding as easily as opening the drawer.

But Eddie loses interest. The insurance policies are like other insurance policies. The coin collection is just that. The photographs are yellowing and show people he's never met nor is likely to ever meet. He has never known his father to have many friends. There are no secrets in this desk. No clues.

A heavy white curtain is drawn to create a separation in the hospital room. E.W. near the bathroom, the teacher laid out under the small porthole of a window. The teacher's daughter and son-in-law sit on plastic chairs at the foot of the bed. Their father's chest heaves, sometimes he gulps for air. His lungs are slowly filling up with mucus. He's drowning, hour by hour, and all that the doctor or anyone can do is watch. Wait until it's over.

E.W. is restless. He tells Eddie that he needs to get home and take Sam for walk. He's worried that no one is looking after the dog.

"Mom's there," Eddie assures him.

E.W. shakes his head. Until now, only he has walked Sam.

"Well, you'll be able to do it again soon," Eddie says, hoping it's true.

E.W. frowns and, for the first time, notices the window. The sky is bleached by a hot sun, the trees milky green.

"The doctor came in yesterday," E.W. says. "He tells the man there are two choices. A lung support system that will keep him alive for another month or two but at great expense and enormous physical pain. The second choice is that nothing be done and nature allowed to take her course. At most, he would have a week."

"That's a choice?"

"Tells him right in front of everyone," E.W. says, pursing his lips. "No consideration. No privacy."

"Was there anyone here besides you?"

"That isn't the point," E.W. snaps.

Eddie stares at the teacher, knowing but unable to grasp that he is watching a man die. He wants to talk to the teacher more than ever, to make friends with his daughter and son-in-law, to unfurl that white curtain and create one big, communal room. But Eddie doesn't move. He fears that everything that needs to be said, begs to be spoken, will never be uttered.

"The Indians had it right," E.W. says. "When it was time to die, they took up their blanket, left the village and walked off into the woods."

"You'd rather be alone when it's your time?" Eddie asks, even though he knows the answer.

Eddie spies the heavy chain lying next to his father's favorite chair. But instead of picking it up and clipping the end to Sam's leather collar, Eddie strolls to the front door, calling for the dog. Sam rouses instantly, leaping from his quiet corner, running for the open door. Eddie laughs as Sam bolts past, hell-bent for a wild, free sprint through the neighborhood.

Eddie slowly closes the heavy door behind them, thrilled to see his father's prized Irish Setter streak up the white sidewalk, past the neat lawns and manicured trees, running with utter abandon. Eddie remembers the last time he let Sam out like this and his father became furious, angry that the dog was loose in the neighborhood and would take hours to retrieve. Eddie listened politely, then shouted Sam's name. As though honoring a secret pact, an agreement that allowed the dog to wander unshackled, Sam soon appeared, streaking around the corner, charging towards home.

Eddie is depending on Sam to obey his call again but, if he doesn't, Eddie will let him roam. E.W. will be home in a few days, walking Sam with his metal leash. The crisis has passed for the moment, his father does not have cancer and the pneumonia is steadily improving.

Eddie strolls up the steep hill toward the woods where he and his friends once played, feeling light and limber. A soft dusk breeze blows, bobbing the tree branches and spreading the scent of freshly cut grass. The smell awakens other summers, times Eddie assumed were long forgotten and he suddenly hears the excited cries of Jeff and Keith and Tommy as though they were just up the street, not moved to other cities and neighborhoods. He can hear them and himself as they chase one another through and around the trees, trying to tag whomever they can reach, reveling in the growing shadows, the approach of nightfall, a time when no one will be calling them for meals or chores or duties. They'll play even after it's dark and the woods fill with the chirping of crickets and cicadas and the faint rustling of wandering birds.

As Eddie turns the corner, however, his sense of joy, of relief, subsides with the breeze. He remembers the teacher, drowning, lying alone in his room, next to a recovering patient too polite to speak. Eddie stops, startled and embarrassed to feel his eyes moisten. But Eddie doesn't cry, will not allow himself to cry. At the same time, Eddie has an overwhelming sense that his life is absurd, a joke. He feels as though he is rolling along like a boat floating on the current, left to drift, disconnected from all that surrounds him. His real self, his genuine feelings and desires, are submerged, sunk so deep that he hardly knows they exist.

"Sam! Sam!" he shouts suddenly. He scans the front yards of the ranch homes, searches all the way up the steep hill where the street lamps have begun to light like fireflies. But the dog doesn't come even after Eddie calls for him another dozen times, his voice echoing through the neighborhood, decaying until it vanishes into the dark, silent yards.

E.W. has a new, private room. There is no window, but his bed faces the door so that he can watch the doctors and nurses and visitors hurrying back and forth on the glistening wax floor.

"Nice digs," Eddie says when he first walks in. He hates it but he knows it's exactly the solitary room his father prefers. The TV hangs just above the door so he can switch back and forth from hospital to movie.

"It's an improvement," his father says. "But the food's still the same."

"I thought you liked the food."

"The desserts are pretty good."

E.W. has been thin his entire life, his body impervious to whatever he feeds it. Eddie can remember the many times that his father would come from work, park himself in front of the TV and devour an entire half gallon of ice cream.

"So when do you have to go back?" his father asks.

"Tomorrow morning. Starting a new project."

"That's good," his father says.

"What do you mean?"

"That you have a new project. It's good to have work, things to keep you busy."

"That's not enough for me," Eddie blurts and his father stops, looking stunned.

"It somehow doesn't feel like it's what I should be doing with my life, nothing does," Eddie continues, fearing that he sounds like a whiner but he can't help himself. He needs direction, someone to help show the way. He needs a father.

"You'll find your way," his father says. "Don't worry so much."

E.W. begins to search his tray, looking for leftovers. There's a chocolate pudding that catches his eye and he picks it up like a child discovering a prize.

"I really appreciate you coming all the way down here to see me," his father says with newfound energy.

"I'm not leaving yet," Eddie says, hating that he can feel himself trembling.

"I know that," E.W. says. "I just wanted to thank you,"

"It would never occur to me NOT to visit you," Eddie says, glaring at his father, more furious than he can ever remember.

"Are you taking the train or driving?"

"The train," Eddie snaps and his voice cracks slightly. "That's how I got here."

"Is there someone to give you a ride to the station?" his father asks.

Eddie nods and, suddenly, he feels the energy rush out of him like a raft pricked by a pin, and he sinks back inside himself, until the anger vanishes and he is staring at a frail, old man who is embarrassed and uncomfortable and would just as soon be left alone.

"Well, I guess I should get going," Eddie says, his voice quiet and subdued. He moves closer to his father until he is touching the narrow bed.

"Give us a call when you get back?" E.W. asks. He pauses, searching his son's face. "You know how your mother worries."

Eddie nods and takes his father's outstretched hand. But it's not until Eddie has passed through the long, bustling corridor and stepped out into the soft, muggy afternoon that he realizes how tightly his father held his hand, how those stern blue eyes shone with something more than fever.

Later, as the train rocks slowly out of the Baltimore station, Eddie remembers the last time he and his father had sailed together. Without a word being spoken, Eddie had assumed the tiller, steering through a narrow channel in the river as E.W. adjusted the main sail. It was autumn and flocks of green-necked mallards congregated on the marsh shore, honking and fluttering in the cool, fading light.

Eddie glimpsed his father in profile, the long, brooding face concentrating, as always, in the execution of his task. But Eddie was startled to see a distinct resemblance, the outline of a man not unlike himself.

VIDEO VERITÉ & OTHER STORIES

Sins of the Father

The night before the scheduled execution, they went to the diner in Huntsville because the TDC officer back at the Polunsky Unit said it had the best home cooking in town. The diner had a corner sign with "Café Texan" painted like the *Wanted: Dead or Alive* posters. Inside, it was vintage south Texas with a Formica lunch counter and ceiling fans and even a soda fountain. Bob appreciated the place was clean, neat, and orderly. The tall plate-glass windows welcomed the rust-colored light of the sunset. It was strikingly beautiful, the sunset. His son had a thing for sunsets. Always was pointing them out, especially when they would go to Padre Island in summer and go fishing on the bayside.

When their meals arrived on heavy white plates, the rims worn but not chipped, Bob was surprised to find that he was hungry. The golden batter that enclosed the sirloin smelled of oil and black pepper and honey. The smooth, thick gravy beckoned with melted butter and cream thickened without the use of corn starch. It was authentic, Bob thought with satisfaction, as he cut into the meat with his steak knife and watched the pungent steam rise from the plate.

"Excuse me," a pretty voice asked. "But are you the Jacobsens?"

Bob immediately wanted to lie and say "no." He and Jane had given interviews to dozens of reporters and TV producers. At first, he had liked talking about it, getting it off his chest, sharing his sadness and his shame. But it wasn't long before the pain and effort of telling the same story over and over became unbearable.

"Do you mind if I sit a minute with you," she said, sitting down before she was finished asking. She had the intense, alert eyes so common among these career women. She had a pretty face, of course, all camera-ready cheekbones and clean lines. Her auburn hair was cut short and sassy like the girls on the shampoo commercials. Bob felt a little intimidated.

"First, let me say how sorry I am," she said in the unaccented English that had become the norm even in Texas. Her clear enunciation also spoke of good schools and money. In fact, she reminded him of a similar beauty he'd known growing up in Denton. She, too, had the breeding that put her beyond reach to a middle-class kid. They might as well have been from different countries.

"I can't even imagine being in your shoes. I don't know what I would be feeling," the woman said.

"Do you have a family, ma'am?" Jane asked her.

"Oh no," the woman said as if that were inconceivable. "My name is Jessica Albert. I'm here doing a story about the Huntsville unit—'The Walls' as they call it." She was about to add something about the monthly, sometimes weekly executions that took place there but stopped herself.

"Nice to meet you, Miss Albert," Jane continued. Bob peered at his wife, annoyed at her being so damn pleasant.

"What network?" Bob snapped.

"TCC," Jessica responded with a slight defensiveness, exposing a vulnerability that both surprised him and made him resent her less. She wasn't perfect. "You know, The Crime Channel. A documentary series called *In Search of Justice*."

Bob nodded trying to remember if he'd ever seen the series or even the channel. There were so many cable stations now, and so many were doing those reality shows that were anything but.

"I'm against what is going to happen tomorrow. It's barbaric," the woman offered.

"Yes, ma'am," Jane said. Bob stared at the perfect piece of chicken fried steak on the end of his fork. He wanted to put it in his mouth but worried how the TV producer might take it.

"You know I talked with your son. Interviewed him, I mean."

Bob started. "Lois Lane" was how his son had described her. He smiled to himself. His son had always had a sense of humor about things. He had told him about that interview, how the woman had cried openly when he told what he did, and how he'd come to understand things in prison with the help of Lord Jesus. Ronnie thought she was real pretty. And smart. Told him she had gone to Yale.

"He's been interviewed a whole lot since the appeal," Bob said.

The reporter nodded, acknowledging that she was, in fact, just one more interviewer. Then she leaned closer to Bob and spoke softly with a familiarity that flattered him.

"You know he did what he did," the woman said. "But your son—he's had eight years on death row and it's changed him—that was clear. He doesn't hesitate to say that he did it. He knows how much pain he has caused both you and the girl's family. He wants to atone."

"Yes ma'am," Jane agreed.

"The state of Texas wants an eye for an eye," she continued. "And your son. Well, he *agrees* with the state. I just don't get that. I just don't. He said to me, 'I deserve this punishment. I was wrong. I took another person's life so I forfeit my own.'"

The woman shook her head and raised her lovely, dark eyebrows in genuine bewilderment. Bob was again reminded of the girl from Denton. How many times had he stared as she strolled effortlessly down the school hallway, her silken dark hair draped over bare shoulders, head held high and mighty like a runway model? Of course, each time she brushed right past him as if he were nothing more than a locker.

"He's a stubborn boy," Jane said. "Always has been. He gets an idea in his head and you can't shake it out of him."

"What do you think, Mr. Jacobsen?" she asked suddenly. He could feel her studying his own face as one might a photograph. He and Ronnie did look alike. The same wide, Slavic face. Ronnie's was thinner with a sprinkle of freckles on cheekbones that were more pronounced. But both had thin, straight hair the color and texture of dry grass. Both were blue-eyed, a cool, impenetrable slate blue. Bob's eyes were further hidden by gold-rimmed aviator glasses that turned a faint gray in bright light like the kind that filled the cafe.

"He believes in the Bible ma'am," Bob answered her question finally. "And he knows it. Studied to be a student minister, you know. He believes in an eye for an eye."

"But he's the eye!" she said, indignant.

"He was almost a minister, you know," Jane said. "He told you about that, right? He told how he was going to be a member of the congregation that summer?"

"Yes," she said. "He did. He said he dropped out at the last minute."

Both Bob and Jane searched her face. The reporter nodded. She had done her homework, Bob realized. But she was kind enough not to speak about it, knowing it didn't help Ronnie's case. Inappropriate advances toward a young woman of a sexual nature, the Bible school had informed them that summer. "The boy was inexperienced," Bob had told them, not so much excusing his son as trying to explain his actions. He didn't have a steady girlfriend. Hadn't all of high school. "I was the same way," he had told the minister. "Didn't get interested in girls until senior year, which is when I met my wife, Jane." Of course, he didn't say anything about that dark beauty from Denton who paid no attention to him. Why would he?

Bob set down his fork reluctantly. He wanted to eat his chicken fried steak. But the reporter was showing no signs of leaving.

"Ma'am," Bob said politely. "We were hopin' to eat dinner here right now."

"Yes, of course, I'm so sorry," the woman said, pretending humility. Bob knew a woman like this usually got what she wanted.

"Would you mind if I talked with you tomorrow on camera? Just a few questions before your son arrives?"

"Sure," his wife said quickly and easily. The woman smiled at them like a neighbor might. Bob wanted to protest, to say they had enough of this talk, but he didn't want to bother Jane, and so he nodded and watched the TV producer stand up, shake their hands, and stroll to the door, elegant and untouchable in her pressed jeans and blue silk blouse.

"Very nice girl," Jane said to him.

"I guess," Bob said, pretending he wasn't impressed. But he resented her too; at least what she represented. Ronnie was a character to these people as were he and Jane. They were being used to tell a story—and willingly so, Bob admitted.

They finished their meal in silence. Bob had lost his appetite, but he ate his chicken fried steak anyway. His wife took a bite or two of her burger and chewed, staring at the plate.

When they finally left Café Texan, the recently installed Victorian streetlamps were on, and the sunset had turned blue and purple like a bruise. They strolled to the car together, holding hands the way they hadn't since they were dating over 30 years ago. The night air was soft and sultry, and it made Bob feel guilty. He imagined his son sitting alone in his bare, crappy cell.

"I don't think I'll be fallin' asleep tonight, Pops," he'd said when their half-hour together was up. "I'll be having plenty of time to catch up." He tried to smile.

They had spent the time talking about everything but what was to happen the next day. Ronnie had repeated his stories about all the friends he had made during his eight years on death row, especially a pen pal from London who had promised to visit but never had.

"Your mother and I will only be thinking about you, son. We love you," Bob had offered, no longer knowing what to say.

Ronnie had smiled at him, his eyes wet, and Bob saw his son at four years old, saying, "Good night. I love you, Pop," just before falling asleep. Bob would watch him as he slept, staring dumbly, bewildered that he could love another person this much.

"What are you thinking about, Bob?" his wife asked, pulling him gently back into the present.

"About this town," Bob said, squeezing her warm hand, not yet weakened with the frailty of age. He didn't want to burden her with more thoughts about their son this night.

The small, turn-of-the-century façades lined the empty street all the way up the hill. There were antique shops, a barber, a clothing store.

There was an unmistakable air of tourism about Huntsville, a careful charm that was tied to luring visitors more than residents. Yet it was a company town where most people worked for the Texas Department of Corrections, helping to run the six maximum security prisons that surrounded the bland outskirts.

"Is that it?" Jane asked, pointing to the brick, fortlike façade of The Walls. "Is that where?"

Bob focused on the round pewter clock that hung over the red-brick entrance to the prison. It was well past six. Less than 24 hours now remained.

"Yes, honey. Yes. That's the place."

Bob braced for his wife's tears, but there was only that dull, dead silence again like the one that had hung over the end of their meal. As they approached their car, he was surprised to feel a twinge of fear that he would soon have to let go of her hand and drive back to that shiny new Holiday Inn Express and wait for morning to see Ronnie.

"I want to go see it," Jane said in a soft voice that veiled her resolution.

"No," Bob said reflexively, knowing that she was going to do as she pleased anyway.

"I want to," she said, gently tugging him.

They took the clean sidewalk across from the row of stores.

"Such nice homes," Jane said as they reached the next block. "I suppose people from the prison must live here, it being so close and all."

The small bungalows, most decades old and some in need of a good paint job, were set along an uneven row. Mesquite and willow oak trees shaded a few of the tiny front yards and gave the block a peaceful air. Just beyond the corner property, the modest red-brick walls of the prison rose up modestly, topped with bales of barbed wire.

A memory forced its way into Bob's mind. He was screaming at little Ronnie at the top of his lungs. The boy wasn't listening to him, defying his orders, and they were trying to leave to get to the grocery store.

"You listen here. Listen!" Bob raged. He suddenly grabbed the boy's little arm, yanked it too hard, and brought him tumbling to the ground. The accident only enraged him more.

"Now listen!"

Ronnie glared back at him, refusing to cry, and Bob grabbed him again. The tears burst forth and the boy welped like a mangy, frightened pup. The sound of his boy's fear pricked his swollen rage and Bob felt it rush out of him like a balloon. He began to cry himself as he picked up his only child and hugged him.

"It's so quiet here," his wife said. "So, so quiet. Ronnie will like that. He always liked quiet places."

"And sunsets," Bob said.

Bob squeezed her hand, hoping his tinted aviators hid the tears welling in his eyes. When police described what his son had done to the girl, Bob said nothing. He listened without visible emotion as they detailed the cigarette burn marks on the girl's lithe body, the gun shot that blew off the side of her head—all still verifiable even though he had doused the corpse and the condo with gasoline and set it on fire. He had been caught by police a few yards away without incident. He had been standing in the dark shadows of the condo complex, watching the blaze and the smoke rise up into the summer night, crying.

Bob never asked his son why he killed the beautiful co-ed. It had happened during final exam week. Ronnie had been pulling all-nighters with the help of various stimulants. He was terrified of underperforming on his tests. This college was his one chance of moving up, joining the Texas elite, the good ol' boys that ran and controlled things. Ronnie told him he went to her apartment to see her. He had asked her out many times and she had politely put him off. She was asleep when he came in through what he claimed was an unlocked door.

"Why did you bring the gun, Ronnie?" Bob had asked.

"I don't know," Ronnie answered.

"Who gave you the handgun?"

"Pops," Ronnie said, shaking his head. "Took it out of the garage when I was home for break."

Bob had bought it at a gun show, getting it for a song as part of a promotion. He'd told himself it might be handy for hunting season or just good to have around the house, just in case there were any problems.

Bob feared he would meet the father of the dead girl again. The father was tall and lean with a long, serious face that radiated trust and integrity. He was a wealthy Dallas banker and devout churchgoer who had stared at him at the trial as if he, not Ronnie, was responsible. Who was worse off, Bob had wondered, staring into space: the father of a convicted killer or the father of a murdered child?

Lois Lane was waiting at a white colonial across from the prison known as the Hospitality House when he and Jane arrived. She jumped from her folding chair and hurried toward him with her bright, dazzling smile leading the way.

"Jessica Albert," she said, reminding them of her name.

She asked if they had heard from the lawyer about Ronnie's appeal. The sound of his son's nickname being spoken aloud, outside of the family, startled and annoyed Bob. He shook his head tersely.

"Well, there's still time," she said. "Can I get you a cup of coffee?"

Bob watched in disbelief as Lois Lane went to the linen-covered table and retrieved two bone-china coffee cups. She was serving them, and it made him feel special, valued, not at all the demon father he feared he was and assumed many believed.

"Cream and sugar?" she asked in a practiced way like a flight attendant.

"Yes, thank you," Jane said. Bob nodded.

"So I'd like to ask you a few questions after you've had a chance to relax," she said, handing first Jane, then himself, the elegant, old china cups. Bob sipped the coffee. Maxwell House. Same thing he drank at home. He looked around the seldom-used living room at the English couches and the Western art on the linen white walls, at the French doors that led to an adjoining room, certain that no one actually lived here. It was a staging room for families who were about to have their son killed by the fair state of Texas.

"I deserve to die, Pops," Ronnie had said to him immediately after the trial. "I killed her. I took her life. I don't deserve mine."

"No one deserves to die," Bob had snapped, feeling that cold trickle of anger chill his spine. "No one."

"I do. I truly do," Ronnie had said, bowing his head as he'd been taught as a student minister.

Of course he had done a horrible thing. There was no bringing back the girl. But revenge—even from the government—it accomplished nothing, atoned nothing. It didn't bring back the dead, right wrongs. Ronnie had never done anything violent before. But his son did have that same quirk as himself, that anger that was as much a part of both of them as their blue eyes.

A bright, white light filled the room. It took Bob a moment to trace the source. One of the young men in the TV crew had turned on a TV light outfitted with an oversized black box made out of cloth and plastic mesh and turned it toward them. Lois Lane was already in front of him.

"What I need to ask isn't easy right now. I know that Mr. Jacobsen. But I have to ask it."

Bob looked at the gleaming wood floors they stood on. He knew what she was going to ask. But he had no answer. No one knew why he murdered the girl. Even Ronnie did not truly know. Maybe the gun was just there to scare her, to give him power over her he did not have. The gun could have went off by mistake as Ronnie had claimed at the trial.

"What I want to ask is about punishment. There's the eye-for-an-eye school and there's the rehabilitate school. The eye for an eye think you punish for punishment's sake. The other school thinks you punish to help reform. Where do you stand?"

Bob almost laughed. A philosophical question. That was easy.

"A little of both, maybe," Bob said. "Depends on the person, I guess. You got to punish people for doing wrong, but you got to help them learn what's right too."

"Have you been that way as a parent?"

"What?" Bob said reflexively, surprised by the sudden turn to the personal.

"Did you punish Ronnie when he did things wrong?"

"Yes," Bob said tersely. "Of course I did. What kind of question is that?"

"Did you ever spank him when he was young?"

"You mean did I ever hit my son? That's what you mean, right? No. I never so much as slapped that boy. I was never violent."

"Never?"

"Never."

She was playing with him, trying to upset him for the camera. He was her toy. But Bob refused. He wanted to tell her about his own dad, but God only knew what the TV people would do with that one. He wanted to tell her, as he had never told anyone—not even Jane—about his father's idea of punishment. He wanted to tell her about the time when he was 12 and he had disobeyed his dad's orders. They had marched to the garage, his father whipping off his belt in silent fury, and stopped at the doorway. Bob stared in disbelief as much as fear. He had never even been spanked by his father. At the last moment, his father had suddenly handed him that thick, black belt, then turned around and raised his shirt to expose his bare back. "I want you to hit me, Bobby. I want you to understand what you caused. This is your punishment. Don't forget it."

"Sir?" the pretty voice asked.

"Yes?" Bob snapped back with the terror of someone who had fallen asleep at the wheel for a moment.

"So what I want to ask is if you agree with your son. Is the death penalty the best form of justice?"

"I believe in the death penalty," Bob said. "There are bad people who just won't or can't respond to prison or any other form of punishment. They can't be stopped."

"So you believe in what's happening here. I mean, if it happens?"

"I didn't say that."

"But you just said you believe..."

"I said I believe in the death penalty," Bob snapped. He glared at the woman, daring her to continue.

"But that means that you are saying its okay for your son."

"I did not say that," Bob said too loudly. He felt his wife's hand on his trembling arm. Bob felt his flushed forehead pounding. He was waiting for someone to move like an alert hunter, tense and dangerously quiet.

"So it's okay for others, but not for your son? Is that what you mean?"

Bob stared at her, feeling the anger rage through him like a drug. He struggled to contain it, not knowing if and how it might take over.

"Honey," Jane whispered. "There's a telephone call for us. It's the lawyer."

Bob nodded. He felt like the morning after a party. He didn't drink much anymore, but there was a time when he drank bourbon all the time. He felt the same kind of weakness and headache and queasiness. Something else rose up within him too, and it shot through him like bile, but exploded in his eyes and he bent over, unable to stop the tears, the weak, sickly warm tears. He was nothing he thought he was. He was weak and tired and growing old.

"I am so sorry," the reporter said, and her voice cracked like an adolescent.

Bob forced himself to stand up, regardless of what he must look like to her and his wife. He met the woman's young and beautiful eyes, glazed with tears of pity. What a piece of work, he thought. Barbaric.

Jane led him away toward an office. A corrections officer was holding the phone. But even before Bob accepted the receiver, he knew. No one in Texas got a stay of execution.

The viewing room was about the size of a walk-in closet. A Plexiglas window looked into the execution chamber. Bob couldn't help but be reminded of the viewing glass at the hospital nursery. Even the walls were painted the faint mint green meant to be soothing. Only the walls inside the chamber were painted over cinder block and a microphone dangled from the ceiling like a stage prop, waiting for a performer to grab it and belt out a tune.

It was silent in the viewing box, and already it smelled of sweat. Jane stood beside him. They held each other's hands so tightly that their palms were drenched. They were anticipating the metal door to the chamber opening and their only son being wheeled into the room on a gurney. Please let him go peacefully, Bob prayed to himself. Let him see us, know that we are here and will always be here for him.

The speaker inside the booth crackled with static followed by the whine of door hinges. Bob stared as the gray entrance door backed away. The gurney was rolling down the cement hallway in front of empty iron holding cells. He recognized his son's bare feet first. Years spent tucking a tiny version of those familiar long, narrow feet with oversized toes into tennis shoes and Dockers. A chore at the time. Always hurried, and Bob resentful, wondering when the baby boy could stand on his own two feet.

Ronnie was smiling and those slate-blue eyes locked into his. Present but far away too. A sheen of glassiness like he'd seen immediately after the arrest. It was the look of someone unable to comprehend. Bob forced himself to not cry, to show no weakness, to do anything that would frighten the boy. Even during Ronnie's final statement, his arm connected to the IVs that would soon fill with saline, then poison, Bob made a show of strength. Ronnie quoted scripture and then turned and said "I love you" right to him just like he always had before going to bed. "I am sorry for the pain I have caused. I am truly sorry."

Even then Bob refused to cry, terrified of frightening the person he loved more than anyone or anything.

The biggest surprise was that Bob felt no anger when it was over. Not at the state, the prison, the warden, not even Lois Lane when she came over and gave him a hug. Ronnie was gone. He could no longer be protected, no longer be controlled for his own good. The responsibility had been lifted from Bob's shoulder, and there was a sense of relief. The powerlessness had sobered him. There was no anger without fear. There was only what was in front of him not whatever ills he might imagine.

"What a waste of human life," Lois Lane said. He heard her talking to her crew who looked vaguely bored, like schoolboys forced to attend yet another class.

Bob held his wife's hand, held it tighter than he should have or meant to.

"Honey, please," she said. "You're hurting me."

Bob let go without apologizing. He marched across the street from The Walls, ignoring the pleas behind him, until he came to the entrance. There was the dead girl's father opening the door to the TDC office building for his wife. He and his wife moved with the patient gentility of the privileged, of people accustomed to being treated with deference. Bob recognized the father's smug, sober glance with its unmistakable air of righteous superiority. Bob had adopted the same pose in countless church services, certain he had a special connection to God.

Now they're both dead, Bob wanted to say. Now we both carry the cross, don't we? Happy now? Yet Bob's certitude had long since dissipated. What meaning can there be in using death to atone death? Yes, the Old Testament promoted an eye for an eye. But death didn't erase sin. It didn't alleviate suffering. It didn't bring back either child.

"We got to get this. GOT TO!"

Bob was startled to see the producer running with her crew like a coach bearing down on hapless players. Her lovely face was contorted with a harsh masculine intensity, her dark eyebrows furrowed demonically as she directed the cameraman to focus on the two fathers. The cameraman was fumbling with the tiny controls on the side of the Betacam.

"Goddamn it Rick, forget the video levels. Just shoot it!"

Her voice rang out over The Walls and everyone—the TDC officers, PR people, other reporters, and especially the fathers—froze for an instant as if captured by a still camera. There was a queer, brief silence that unnerved Bob. Before he knew it, the father had vanished into the building, followed by a trio of TDC officers in their confederate gray uniforms.

"Enough," Bob yelled, glaring at the camera, and then bolting toward the girl, his neck pulsing, his head pounding, feeling nothing but rage. Rage at the senselessness, the callowness, the indifference. He was mere fodder, an object to be used and shaped like his son to make an example.

Bob came within an instant of grabbing her, but in the end, he couldn't.

"That's enough, miss," Bob said finally, struggling to see through the sudden blurring of his vision. These people were like jackals. "That's enough."

Lois Lane hesitated, letting the jackals get off a few more seconds of tape before she softly ordered him to stop.

Bob turned and walked steadily back to his wife. His anger vanished as swiftly as it had appeared. There was no sense to it. Ronnie was gone. The banker's girl was gone. No past mistakes were rectified, no sins forgiven. Playing God, Bob thought, only showed how helpless we were.

Yet Bob felt a sickening guilt. Guilt for all he did not do for his son, all he couldn't do. His only son had died for the sins of the father as much as the boy's own violent crime. Ronnie had been born and raised in the shadow of a world that was always just beyond his reach.

Bob and his wife walked back inside The Walls where a lone officer waited. The man nodded stoically—like a soldier, Bob thought as they approached. He would march them to retrieve their son's body so that he could be driven home to Denton for a proper Christian burial—Ronnie's last and only request.

Telling Time

One of the most effective ways to lie is to tell the absolute truth. Jake discovered this fact the morning his wife noticed his new wristwatch. As he followed her suspicious eyes to the elegant Olde English script sheathed under the flawless crystal, Jake knew that he'd committed one of those thoughtless errors he'd always read about in mystery novels or detective fiction, the kind where the criminal is caught because of a small, seemingly insignificant detail. But Jake did not give in to his panic. He took a short, sudden breath and explored a new realm of honesty.

"Christmas present from my mistress," Jake said.

"She's very generous," Cynthia answered, her tone of voice equally casual. She smiled with her lips and Jake did the same. It seemed to Jake if they were flirting. But then Cynthia's hand shot across the table and grabbed his wrist. Instinctively, he tried to escape her grasp but she held on, tenacious as always.

"This is very well made," she said, studying the timepiece. Cynthia was an illustrator with the kind of artistic training that made her especially keen to visual detail.

"It reminds me of your old watch, the one that I gave you for your birthday. The Hamilton that you left in the laundry bag one day," she said, shaking her head the way a mother might dismiss her truant son.

"I left it in the pocket of my jeans," Jake said.

"You can't hold on to anything," she said. "You lose everything."

"I don't lose everything."

"It's amazing," his wife continued as if she hadn't heard him. "You're so absentminded."

He and his wife were separated by her butcher block table. All the furniture and kitchenware in their new apartment belonged to his wife except for the heavy white mugs, steaming with the sweet caramel scent of their morning coffee. The mugs were among Jake's most prized possessions, the last remaining artifacts of his long bachelor hood.

"What are you doing tonight?" Cynthia asked later as she was preparing to leave for work. She slipped on her tiny leather gloves, not looking at him, suddenly shy.

Jake studied her dark suede overcoat that stretched to her ankles. He thought it was a fashion better suited to a taller, thinner woman. The coat made his petite wife look like a kid wearing her mother's jacket. Jake was embarrassed by her appearance and he wondered if this sudden dislike was a sign, one of those subtle clues that would tell him whether or not he had married the right person. It was a doubt that had lingered since the beginning.

"I haven't made any plans. Are you working late again?"

"Not too late," Cynthia said. Jake could hear the pleading in her voice but it didn't move him. He felt outside of it, outside of himself.

"Let's talk later," he proposed.

Jake listened to the door slam behind her, to the racket of her heels as she rushed down the long, parquet hallway and opened the heavy iron door that led to the street. It was at that moment that Jake suddenly snapped off the watch, hating it, hating that he was wearing it, hating that he was so vain to have kept it. He jammed it into the pocket of his blue jeans and left for the office.

As he hurried down the gray sidewalk, past the stench of the drifting trash along upper Broadway, anxious to reach the subway, he pictured the evening Mira had given him the watch in her sleek, modern suite, apologizing in advance, saying she knew it was inappropriate but she couldn't help herself. She'd spotted the watch at Bloomingdale's and "just knew" it would look perfect on him. The presumption that she might know his personal tastes, what he really loved and didn't love, had infuriated him into a stone cold silence.

"Did I upset you?" she asked, genuinely concerned.

"How could you buy a wristwatch? What were you thinking?" Jake asked.

"I just saw it and wanted you to have it. I didn't think about other people."

"This has got to stop," Jake said.

"I'll return it," Mira said. "Or you can give it to a friend. It doesn't matter to me."

"I'm not talking about the watch," Jake said.

"I'll get you something else," Mira said. She had heard his threat to quit the affair before.

"How much did this cost?" Jake asked, studying the watch.

"I don't know," Mira said. "I charged it."

She waited for him from her perch on the warm bed, her naked legs curled up underneath like a cat, wrapped in her black lace mistress costume, the kind of cheesy lingerie that he'd seen on the models that sprawled across 900-number ads. He glanced through the window behind her at the vast, brazen lights of Manhattan pulsing like a Times Square marquee. Later, after they had sex, he had taken a long, scalding shower, staying under the roaring nozzle until his chest burned red.

Jake was relieved to get to work and think about something else. He and Steve, his longtime editor, were making selections from a recent corporate video shoot that Jake had produced. The footage was of talking heads, high level corporate executives discussing the future of their company. Jake evaluated the quality of the footage, having Steve cut anything out that was poorly lit, a defect that would make the executives look bad. At the same time, Jake listened for sound bites that he could use when it came time to do the final edit.

But today Jake saw and heard something different, or thought he did. He worried that it was just his agitated state of mind. The ruddy faced Irish CEO was discussing the need for the insurance company to get leaner and meaner and more competitive. The only way to accomplish this important task, he promised with a look of grave sincerity, was to downsize. The CEO planned to have thousands of loyal employees, workers who had given ten or fifteen years of their lives to the company, simply disappear, discarded like empty cartons. He assured his audience, the people he was throwing away, that the firings were essential if the company was to remain profitable. Jake did not doubt that this was true. But he wondered suddenly if it wasn't something of a lie too, a greed so brazen, so honest that no one questioned it.

Jake watched the camera tilt down to reveal the watchband on the wrist of the talking head, glinting like gold tooth fillings under his starched white cuff.

"Do you think that's even a real Rolex?" Jake wondered aloud.

"Yeah. Of course it's real," Steve said.

"How can you tell?"

"Because these guys can afford one."

Jake laughed, remembering the watch stuffed in his black jeans. He slid it carefully out of his front pocket, checking the door as if he were afraid that some detective would suddenly burst through and arrest him. Jake set it down under the tiny reading light by the sound board.

"You want this watch?" Jake asked.

Steve leaned closer to examine it. Jake did the same as if Steve might find something he had not. The elegant, old world design seemed quaint in the amber glow of the sound levers, the red digital counters, the electronic green edit list pulsating on the inlaid computer screen. The watch, Jake thought, was from another world, another time, another way of seeing. It was from his father's time, a time when a man worked for one company for life, married one woman for life—as his father had—when sudden firings of loyal employees were as rare as divorces and equally deemed a last resort.

Steve started laughing in a way that made Jake feel foolish, naive.

"They got you, huh?" he said, finally. "They conned you with this knock off and now you're trying to get me."

"What are you talking about?" Jake asked, suddenly unsure.

Steve spun around in his swivel chair and gave him a sidelong glance, his thick eyebrows arched comically. He was a dark, stocky Italian, raised on the streets of Bensonhurst. He believed no one.

"Why do you want to get rid of it?"

"I don't like it," Jake said. "It's not me."

Steve grinned, a hearty grin that showed his pink gums.

"That's totally you," he said, glancing at Jake's clean, boyish face and short, wavy hair. Except for the deepening wrinkles at the corner of his blue eyes, he could have been mistaken for a recent Yale graduate.

"It's an executive's watch," Steve said. "Esquire-y. Expensive-looking. Even for a knockoff."

Steve chuckled and spun around to operate the edit console. Jake jumped out of his chair and stalked out of the dark edit room. Moments later, he found himself marching under an ashen sky on West 57th Street, the wind gusting uphill, off the Hudson River, scratching his cheeks. He turned away, hurrying toward the nearest subway. Halfway down the block, he realized he'd rushed out of the studio without his down ski jacket and wore only a denim shirt, unbuttoned at the neck. Still, he couldn't turn around, go back.

Jake spotted a tall, coal-black Senegalese, wrapped in tattered old blankets, a rainbow African hat crowning his head. He stood just beyond the subway grating, steam billowing from the underground. An open black briefcase was at his sandaled feet, crammed with watches. Jake hurried toward him, through the metallic tasting steam, and stooped down to examine the knock off watches. It took him less than a minute to find a copy of his watch, flawless down to the brand insignia. Only the cheap, black vinyl strap gave the copy away.

"How much?" Jake asked.

Steve was lounging in his swivel chair when Jake rushed back into the dark edit room, his editor's legs propped up on the lighted console. He was talking in a low, subdued voice on the telephone, Jake's watch lying in the palm of his hand. Jake set the fake watch on his open palm, next to the real one. Steve continued to whisper on the phone. The coy, romantic secrecy irritated Jake.

"Feels like a block of ice," Steve said, dropping the phone on the hook.

"Who was on the phone?" Jake asked. Steve laughed off the question.

"They could both be knock offs," Steve said, comparing the watches. "You really want to get this off your hands, don't you?"

"You want it or not?" Jake demanded.

"Why don't you just return it?" Steve asked. "Get all your money back instead of selling it to me."

"It was a gift."

"So get the receipt."

"I can't."

Steve's expression changed, a sudden seriousness that made Jake feel exposed even though there was no way he could have known who had given him that wristwatch. But there was something in his manner, an excessive thoughtfulness that made Jake regret showing him the watch at all.

"Forget it," Jake said, reaching for the watches.

"I like this one with the black band," Steve said. "Give you fifty bucks."

"What's wrong with the real one?"

"I don't like it either."

Jake fought a strange, sickening panic. The watch had suddenly acquired a life of its own, like a voodoo doll. He felt like it was strapped to him, wedded to him in a strange, dark way. Sitting in the darkened edit room, surrounded by the electronic glow of control buttons, he again felt that same sense of heightened reality, the druglike trance of feeling outside of himself as he had that evening at Mira's suite.

A sudden, desperate urge made him call Cynthia. Before he even said hello, he asked her to dinner, ready to plead if necessary, ready to do anything, anxious to clear himself.

"But I am going to be working late," she said, reminding him of their conversation that morning.

"That's fine," Jake said. "We'll eat late."

There was a long pause. He could hear the background chatter of people in her office, the steady thump of a Xerox machine, spouting out copies. "Are you OK?" she asked. "You sound strange."

"If you had to listen to corporate spin doctors all morning, you'd sound strange too."

Jake and Steve worked on the video until long after the offices closed, much later than they expected. The work of choosing pictures and sound bites absorbed them and neither mentioned the watch again, not until they were leaving the building, now empty except for the all night security guards. Jake had never realized that there were so many. They seemed to be at every entrance and elevator in the entire building.

"Man, there's just no way to tell," Steve said, studying his new watch.

During the long taxi ride back to his neighborhood, Jake stared at the passing buildings as if they were walls. He felt hemmed inside a maze, a labyrinth utterly of his own making, his own confusion. He did not know what to believe anymore.

After the driver pulled to a stop in front of his apartment, Jake pulled the watch out of his pocket, along with the money to pay him. Impulsively, he made a decision. He was finally just going to get rid of the Esquire watch. The only reason it haunted him, he decided, was because he allowed it to. No one was accusing him of anything. No one knew.

"Here's your tip," Jake said, handing him the watch. The driver, a middle-aged Chinese man, shook his head and smiled the way Jake had seen the Chinese do in his favorite restaurant, a gesture that hid more than it told.

"These no work," the driver said. "No work."

"Keep it," Jake said. "Do whatever you want with it." The driver smiled that smile.

Jake slammed the car door and slipped dumbly out onto the dark street, watching the battered yellow cab drive away, loathing the driver. A stark, cold silence settled in its wake. There was no one on the streets. It was too cold, too harsh a winter night. Jake stood still, admiring the floodlit entrance to his home as if it were a work of art.

The apartment was dark, smelling of Cynthia even though she was not yet home. Jake didn't bother turning on any lights and walked over to the telephone answering machine on the white kitchen counter. The red message light was blinking and Jake knew it was Cynthia even before he pressed the retrieve button and listened to his wife's plea to call her at work. She was apologetic, saying how sorry she was over and over again but that the client had called at the last minute and wanted something changed. She was going to be late.

Jake collapsed on the couch, suddenly overwhelmed with fatigue. He sat in the dark living room, listening to the faint, lonely hum of the refrigerator. A wall clock clicked from its perch on the wall. Jake considered leaving but he couldn't move, couldn't do anything. Sometime in the midst of this lethargy, he heard the key in the door lock, the loud creak of it opening and saw the light from the hallway spill into the apartment. The dark figure, draped in a long cape that reached to the floor, rustled past him.

"Cynthia?"

His wife screamed, her hands crossing her chest and neck. Her naked, instinctive fear startled both of them.

"Jake? What are you doing? You scared the life out of me," she said, trying to catch her breath. "Why are you sitting in the dark?"

"I couldn't get up," he answered.

Cynthia turned on the brass reading lamp next to the couch. Jake winced from the sudden burst of light. He squinted at his wife who stood above him, worried, her dark eyes examining him like a nurse.

"Are you going to tell me what is going on?" she asked, her voice edged with frustration. "I wish you'd tell me the truth."

Turn Around

James squinted through the blurry windshield wanting to see just how hard it was raining. He didn't care about getting wet when he stepped out of her car, about spending the next six hours crammed into a narrow airline seat, shivering coast to coast from the dampness and the chill cabin air. He just needed to see how bad it was—the way people stop at automobile accidents. Stephanie broke the silence, a silence that had sat between them during the long ride through industrial L.A., the windshield wipers marking time like a toneless metronome.

"I'll go inside with you," she said, simultaneously pressing the trunk release button on the floor of the rental car. She was a practical woman. James nodded, stealing a glimpse of the rain as it fell past one of the tall street lamps, silent and beautiful in a way he couldn't explain.

James was drenched the moment he pulled himself out of the car and stepped onto the black pavement, which glistened like polished slate. He ignored the sharp, prickly rain on his neck, the water trickling under and through his T-shirt. He strolled to the back of the car and yanked his heavy bag out of the trunk in one smooth motion. Absently he wondered if those long, dull months at the gym weren't finally amounting to something. He was getting leaner, stronger, more fit than he'd ever been.

Stephanie joined him on the black tarmac as the pneumatic glass doors swung out to greet them, the two walking side by side into the bright acoustics of the airline terminal. They stopped nearly at the same moment, as if arriving at the end of a formal procession. James noticed that she had hardly been touched by the rain. Even her long, sandy hair was barely misted on top along the dark middle crease where she parted it. The fact that she had so sensibly taken care of herself annoyed him and he felt himself go cool, the competitive, challenging cool, the preparation for a contest.

Stephanie's calm demeanor nearly derailed him. She seemed so calm as to be bored, her long, smooth face expressionless, the delicate lips curled with a slight impatience. James imagined that she had been through many scenes like this, escorting lovers to their exit. He imagined she was relieved to see him finally leave, even though he himself had staged enough of these scenes to know better. But he was conscious only of that endless walk on the gray beach in Santa Monica during what would have been a brilliant sunset on a clearer day, when she told him she wanted to be alone, that she wasn't ready to get involved with anyone.

James made the first move. He stepped toward her and pecked her on the cheek. He knew what he was doing and when he felt her stiffness as he performed the expected hug he sensed that he had hurt her, that she had hoped to say good-bye as friends. But he was happy to deny her that indulgence, had wanted her to feel as rejected as he did.

James found it easy, then, to turn about face and march along the red carpet to the airline counter, ignoring the vague urge to glance back and watch her slip away through the glass exit doors. He felt he had dismissed her and as he handed over the ticket envelope to the waiting attendant, he was already creating plans for his life back in New York. Imagining these new possibilities, he felt a surge of freedom, of the thrill of having no one to answer to or to explain himself.

But as the attendant patiently scrolled the computer screen, searching for one of the few available seats, James felt a sickening wave of doubt, of fear, a sudden, physical queasiness. There had been a special feeling between he and Stephanie, a warm, intimate familiarity that was wildly out of proportion to lovers who had known each other for less than a month. Each kiss, he remembered, each effortless embrace, every eager conversation had possessed an immediacy unlike any he had ever known. There had never been any doubt in his mind that this rare kinship promised a future, some kind of future.

"Got one," the attendant sang out. She smiled, proud to have mined a seat for him. Her long, graceful fingers tapped through a maze of commands with swift efficiency. James liked her easy bustle, her clear sense of purpose as the printer sounded off, rattling a paper copy of his new seat assignment.

It was at this very moment, as he admired her professional detachment, that James had an instinctive urge to turn away. He did so immediately, without thinking, the way animals do.

Stephanie stood a foot away from him, her soaked hair flattened against her ears, rain still dripping from her narrow chin. Her light green eyes, speckled with gold, gazed at him, wide and unblinking; big, fearful eyes. She stood perfectly still, composing herself. She seemed smaller to him, seemed even thinner in her long summer dress than she already was, enveloped in a sheer innocence that made her appear to be a teenager, not a woman his age.

"I made a U-turn," she said, finally, her voice so soft that he had to strain to hear her. "I couldn't leave. I tried. I really tried. But then I saw that damn U-turn sign."

A slight, coquettish smile followed and as James held her, pulling her closer, collapsing around her, he felt a surge of life rush back into him, a sudden clarity as if waking from a dream.

VIDEO VERITÉ & OTHER STORIES

The Perfect View

They stood on the floating dock with a handful of other intrepid tourists, waiting for the park ranger to finish her instructions. Paul searched the ice-blue water that surrounded them for the flash of a striped bass or one of the red snappers that were said to be common in the pristine inlet.

"So, set your watches," the park ranger said, only half kidding. She was tall with wide, masculine shoulders that were equal to his, which made Paul think she might be a climber.

"It is 9:12 a.m. At five, I'll be back to pick everyone up. Until then, you have the island to yourselves," the ranger continued. Her voice was lighter, more traditionally feminine than her physique.

"What if someone is late?" Amy asked. Paul smiled at her question, both because of her habitual tardiness and what he perceived as the unnecessary bluster of the park ranger. After college, Paul had spent two years teaching rock climbing in the Italian Dolomites and never once tried to scare his students into complying with his orders. But that was the government for you.

"Don't be late," the park ranger said.

"You would leave us here?" Amy insisted.

Paul felt a twinge of embarrassment. Next to the local park ranger, whose boxy uniform draped over a surprisingly lean, taut body, Amy looked like the pampered city girl on a *Survivor* episode.

"Amy," he said, catching the sexy green eyes of the park ranger.

"They're not going to leave anyone out here."

Paul wouldn't have been displeased if they did. He was at home in the wilderness and the less people to spoil it, the better. If they were forced to spend the night here, the only danger was the relative cold of late summer in Downeast Maine.

"Just don't be late, ma'am," the ranger said.

Paul put his arm around Amy's small, sinuous waist and watched the tall, redheaded park ranger climb gracefully into the boat. At the last moment, he caught her glancing back at him or at the group, he wasn't certain. The deckhand pushed off and the boat chugged away, its wake causing the dock to sway and bob on the glassy water. Amy leaned against Paul for balance.

"What a blue," Amy said, seeing the water for the first time. "It's somewhere between a marine and cobalt but totally saturated."

Paul stooped down and put his hand in the water. The ranger had claimed the coastal water was so cold that it could bring about hypothermia within a minute to someone unlucky enough to fall in.

"Is it really cold?" Amy asked.

"Like ice."

"The boat's already gone," one of the tourists said. His voice had the acoustic clarity of a recording studio in the utter silence left in the boat's wake. Paul marveled at the technical effect, one that for a strange, uncomfortable moment reminded him of work and the city he and Amy had only recently escaped.

"That woman was a wack job," Amy said, following the distant cabin of the boat as it drifted out of view. "Do you really think the Park Service would leave someone behind, Paul?"

His girlfriend's voice was also studio-quality, a fact that reminded him that the other tourists would hear every word distinctly, whether they wanted to or not.

"I doubt it," Paul said, playing to his larger audience. "Isle au Haut is part of Acadia National Park. If they left anybody behind, it would be a scandal."

"She had beautiful green eyes," Amy said. "The color of lichen."

"I bet she's a climber," Paul said. "She's got the build."

"Are those the kind of sweet young things you used to train in Italy?" Amy teased.

"No, they were cuter," Paul said.

"I wouldn't have known, the way you were checking her out," Amy said, playfully pinching his arm.

They strolled down the gently drifting dock. The others had already reached the shore that was shaded with towering, dense evergreens. Paul was only too happy to take time leaving the dock. If they were lucky, the other tourists would disperse by the time they arrived at the shore. He wanted the outdoors all to himself, in complete, unblemished solitude.

"I'm so happy we decided to take this trip," Amy said, suddenly exuberant. Her impulsiveness still managed to take him by surprise. He instinctively pulled her closer.

"Nothing like a little nature to help you get a new perspective on things," his girlfriend added.

Amy, he knew, liked nature because she loved to paint abstract landscapes, and the outdoors offered an endless source of colors and shapes. Paul liked the outdoors for its purity, its rejection of all that was man-made. He tolerated living in the city because it was where he made his living. His dream, however, was to build a sound studio in the country where he could do all his post-work far from midtown Manhattan.

Once they reached the shore, they followed the path up the incline, where it led through more of the towering coastal evergreens. The path was cushioned with a bed of fallen green and gold needles. The air was pungent with the scent of both the ocean and the pine, heated by the hot summer sun. Soon, they emerged into the sunlight and found themselves near the edge of a granite cliff. Isle au Haut, the High Island as the French explorers named it.

"We should be able to do this trail in a day," Paul said, examining the trail that wound ahead of them. "In fact, it might not even take that long."

"We don't have to hike the whole trail, Paul."

"Why not?"

"There is just so much to see, to take in. I'd love to just sit and sketch this place."

"Sit?" Paul said.

"Just for a little while. Can we?"

A few minutes later, they came upon an outlook that was even more expansive than the first. Amy stood, staring wordlessly at the horizon. Then, without warning, she found a comfortable perch on one of the massive boulders, pulled her sketchpad and tin box of oil sticks out of the rucksack and started to work. Paul stood helplessly alongside her. He followed her small, girlish hand as it traced the shifting blues of the vast sea, the pearly sky, the evergreens clinging to pewter cliffs.

"We can't stop so soon," Paul said.

"It's a gorgeous view," Amy said.

"We could stop later."

"But the light will change, Paul. It won't be the same."

Paul gazed up at the overcast sky, flat and featureless as an empty piece of paper. There was no way he was going to simply sit here and watch. She knew he wasn't capable of it.

"I want to keep going," Paul said.

"Uh-huh."

"Well I can't just sit," Paul pleaded, like it was a genetic flaw, behavior beyond his control.

"Maybe you should go, then."

"I want you to come with me." Paul startled himself with the direct request. He was usually vague when it came to asking what it was he wanted from her.

"Oh, Paul. Relax. Stay with me."

"I'm going to hike, the way we planned."

"Go for it," Amy said, her center of attention now focused solidly on the vast, empty sea in front of them.

Paul pressed his lips together in silent protest before he marched off, retracing the path that had taken them to the outlook until it hooked up with the only trail on the island. The restlessness that he'd felt as soon as they arrived at the airport was back and more unsettling than ever. He wanted to be here and yet he didn't. He wanted to hike but not like this. It wasn't quite the way he imagined.

Nevertheless, Paul threw himself into the solo hike, embracing the chilly, brine-scented wind that tousled his curly hair and caused his white T-shirt to flap madly like a sail loosened from its halyard. The path followed the twists and turns of the adjacent cliffs, and he found himself gazing frequently out to the rolling blue swells of the Atlantic. There was a very faint, guttural hum to the waves, the groan of a massive undercurrent.

"You know what I love about you?" Amy had said on the plane as it banked over the same ocean and made its approach into the Blue Hill airport. "The fact that you are so exacting, that you want to get everything just right. I'm like that, at least with my painting."

Paul had continued looking out the window, afraid her allusion to his sound work was nothing more than a step board to talk about their relationship again, encroaching on what was their first vacation together in over a year. He'd already begun to regret proposing it, aware that friends, family, and time itself—he would turn 35 in the winter—raised certain expectations about their impromptu getaway, expectations that he did his best to ignore.

"And you know what scares me about you?" Amy continued. She waited until he finally turned to face her.

"What?" he asked. He tried not to smile but those silken brown eyes, speckled with a deep indigo, met his with such fierceness, such affection, that he feared falling in love with her all over again.

"What scares me is that you are never satisfied, that you always want everything to be perfect. And nothing is perfect."

"Don't be scared," Paul said, smiling. He was anxious to steer the conversation to something less personal.

"Do you love me?"

Paul groaned inwardly. He was immediately aware of the passengers that were crammed in around them.

"Amy," he whispered. "Look where we are."

"In an airplane?"

"Can we talk about this later?"

"I'm just asking you what you are feeling. Is that so difficult?"

Paul nodded, sensing his face flush slightly, much like the first time he'd gone to a Sunday dinner with Amy's family, and heated arguments broke out among her siblings before even an appetizer was served. He'd been startled by the outburst, in part because of the contrast with his own family, where emotions were distrusted and conversation more often masked feelings than expressed them.

"Of course I love you. Can't we just enjoy one another, Amy? Do we have to make a big stink about it?"

"I like big stinks," Amy said, adding that bright, girlish laugh he adored. At the same time, he noted her curious pushiness, the way she always seemed poised to interrogate him about his feelings when they ought to have been as obvious as day. It was another black mark against her in that growing, unacknowledged list he was compiling in his mind.

Paul came to a sudden, instinctive halt. The trail had come to an abrupt end. He was virtually at the edge of the cliff, and the path had vanished literally into thin air. So, he concluded with a slow-burning anger, the trail does not circle the island as promised. There wasn't going to be an all-day hike, with or without Amy.

Defiant, Paul immediately decided he was not going to be stopped. He was also not going to return to Amy's perch and laze alongside her like a puppy dog. Just below his feet, before the cliff face plummeted hundreds of stories—so steep that the crash of the waves against the distant breakers was barely discernable even to Paul's trained ears—he noted a series of indentations that could help him descend. There was some risk, but nothing he hadn't seen in his climbing days, even if those college days were 15 years past. In any case, he was certain it was better to keep moving, go somewhere.

The footholds were even better than he anticipated. Paul moved nimbly down the granite outcrops as if he were descending a ladder. The exertion got his blood pumping and before long he was feeling elated—that familiar climbers' high—and he luxuriated in it. He couldn't have wished for a better antidote to his recent frustrations. With a sudden, unexpected clarity, he also understood what was troubling him most. Amy wanted something from him that he could not give. He had been truthful on the airplane. He did love her. But he had always imagined himself married to a different kind of woman.

Paul was forced to stop. At first, he assumed it was a passing problem. Climbers often had to pause and reevaluate their foot- and handholds. But his experience told him what he was slow to accept. There were no footholds, only flat, sheer rock face. He would have to turn around. But as he did so, Paul also recognized a mistake. He hadn't been paying close attention to his climb for the last few movements and, not surprisingly, he had committed the kind of error that was common to green climbers.

Paul didn't get angry with himself. He was feeling too good. But he wasn't going to be able to return the way he had come. The foothold was too far away. He turned and pressed his back against the wall, careful not to look down and risk vertigo. He stretched his leg out like a stick, jabbing for a foothold again but felt only air as his foot dangled weightlessly in the wind. He searched the rock face above him, guessing that his best route was climbing higher, not sideways as he had come.

But the granite was worn as smooth as an antique pewter bowl. The only possible niche was about three feet from his outstretched arm. It was covered in deep green lichen. Most moss could not survive the weathering on slick, sheer rock; a fact that suggested it hid a small divot upon which it clung to survive. What Paul didn't know was whether it was a small fingerhold or something larger that would actually support his weight. It was a terrible unknown because he knew he would have to jump to reach the moss and if it were merely a fingerhold, it would be like trying to grip a glass pane and there would be nothing between him and the distant breakers but the whine of the offshore wind.

Paul glanced anxiously below him. He was at least as high as a skyscraper. Instead of a balance-destroying vertigo, however, he discovered a sudden, mild elation. The blue swells rolled toward the dark, tombstone breakers with a majesty that was inspiring. He could jump, Paul said to himself, holding back a laugh. He could just jump. It wouldn't be difficult to get out beyond the breakers. Forget the niche. Just jump. It would be liberating. Let go, give in to fate, to luck, to God, to whatever force controlled the future.

But when Paul looked back to the rock face above him, his elation vanished. He knew better. The impact of the fall alone would collapse his lungs and possibly snap a rib or two. Even if he did manage to maintain consciousness, the bitter cold of the water would entomb him in an ice block that would sink long before he tried to swim out of the clutch of the jagged, monolithic breakers.

Paul began to berate himself for getting into such an amateur predicament. In all his early years of climbing, he had never been in the kind of danger he had stumbled into now. It was the cost of losing focus, of letting the mind wander. How often had he repeated the mantra during instruction? Focus, focus, focus.

Now this. If the moss above him was concealing a niche, his fingers would slide off the bald rock face and he would be gone. The wind would muffle any cry he uttered, and the distant lobster boat—which he now spotted bobbing on the water like a bathtub toy—would be an unlikely witness. He would vanish into anonymity until his battered body washed up with the empty mussel shells.

Amy would be stricken. He knew it in his gut. She had invested herself in him, given her best self without evident fear, holding nothing back. He marveled at her courage, her willingness to commit. Hesitation and doubt were utterly crushed by her impulsive, hopeful energy, and it carried them both.

Paul felt the resolve fill his legs and his arms, a sudden solidity, as though he had passed from a narrow ledge to a wide swath of rock-hard cement. His mind was clear, untroubled. He knew what he had to do. It was coldly, unmercifully simple. He jumped.

The niche was even deeper than he had hoped. His fingers ripped through the damp lichen and locked onto the side of the rock. Paul ground his uneven teeth as he slowly pulled his dead body weight up. He swung himself sideways and dug his right boot into a crevice. Another was nearby. Paul forced himself to exhale to keep his muscles limber, his body pliable. Swiftly, nearly effortlessly, he climbed up to the ridge, darting in and out of footholds and handholds like the climbing ace he once was.

Paul let out a whooping cry at the summit. He'd beaten the mountain. He'd saved himself. His eyes were drawn to the lobster boat which had pulled up its anchor and was now cutting a small route farther out to sea. He could see a few men in yellow rainslickers, facing his mountain. Maybe they had seen him after all; a minute dab on the cliff face like those tiny, white dots Amy placed on the dark, flat irises of her portraits to make them appear to gleam with life.

Within minutes, Paul was back where he started. He stood at the edge of the path, watching Amy. She was sitting cross-legged, her body arched slightly over her sketchpad, drawing the scene from Isle au Haut.

"The most difficult thing is learning how to see," Amy had told him a few weeks after they had started dating. They had slept together on their third date and had done so nearly every night since. "The drawing is easy. It's seeing what's truly in front of you that takes time and effort."

Paul saw her as a portrait suddenly, a young woman sitting near the edge of a cliff, her long black hair rustling like leaves in the wind. Beyond her were a still, slate sky, and a blue, sometimes black, sea. Both stretched effortlessly to the horizon but never met. The image disturbed him the way too much time alone sometimes did, but there was something indescribably beautiful too, a composition that suggested balance, a natural, edifying harmony.

Paul found he was unable or unwilling to move. He stood silent, mute. For the first time in a long time, he felt at peace with himself. He was content to stand and observe and take in what was clearly a perfect view.

VIDEO VERITÉ & OTHER STORIES

A Woman in Green

His burly roommate strolled into the living room of the duplex and presented the chalk-white pills in the palm of his hand. They looked like Tylenol tablets. Peter waited for the explanation, but he knew it would have something to do with better health through vitamins. His roommate never missed an opportunity.

"Niacin, P-man. Improves blood circulation and the ability of the red cells to breathe," Mangianelli said. "And, if taken hours before, improves the stiffness and performance of the member."

"The member," Peter repeated.

"Try it," he said.

"Why?"

"There has to be a reason for everything?"

Peter stared at the familiar gap-toothed grin spreading across his roommate's face. The salesman's charm made Peter laugh in spite of himself. He'd already gone this far with Mangianelli and his ideas, what was one more?

"So when's this niacin kick in, anyway, Mangia?" Peter asked after washing down the pills with a shot of tap water. The city tap water, he was reminded again, was infused with so much chlorine that it tasted like water from a swimming pool.

"Depends on the physiology," Mangianelli said.

"What's that in minutes, professor?"

"Half hour to an hour, maybe. Could be more."

Back in his room, Peter finished gathering his khaki shorts, Gap T-shirts, surfer trunks, and Teva sandals, preparing for summer. It was another brown Dallas winter, but by the afternoon he would be standing underneath the leafy palm trees of the Yucatan. When he had told Annie about their plans to hang out for a weekend—just the boys—she had tersely reminded him that Cancun was a pre-fab paradise, trucked in on flatbeds and barges, founded, like Las Vegas, on a profit scheme. The Mexican government had used a supercomputer to find the sunniest, most accessible strip of undeveloped land in the country, a coastal paradise to transform into a profitable resort.

"So?" Peter retorted.

"It's so not you, Peter. You're going to be miserable."

"It's only two days, Annie. And I promised Mangianelli I'd do this with him. It's important for his relationship. You know, with Leslie."

"With Leslie?" she said, dismissively. "He's just looking for an excuse. You can see it a mile away. They've broken up how many times now?"

"Annie. He loves Leslie. They're just working things out. He told me." Peter had his doubts, but out of loyalty, he took his friend's earnest statements at face value.

"So why not fly to Big Bend, go hiking?"

"Cancun is where he wanted to go. And you know how easy it is to get a seat on that Saturday morning flight as a non-revenue."

"And you have no vote? There's plenty of places you can fly non-rev. That's the beauty of working for the airlines, right?"

"Don't worry about it."

"I just don't understand why you need to do this."

Peter refused to recognize her jealousy and distrust. Mangianelli had laughed when he told him about the conversation with Annie.

"Hey. We're not married, P-man," he said.

"True," Peter acknowledged.

"And P-man, just because you're on a diet, doesn't mean you can't look at the menu."

Peter finished laying out his beach clothes and hopped into the shower. The warm water shooting from the Waterpik was immediately soothing. He had slept at Annie's apartment the night before and hurried out in the morning without showering. He didn't want her to start pestering him again and somehow persuade him to call off the boys' weekend.

Peter's chest and face suddenly exploded, the skin burning as if splashed with acid. He jumped out of the shower, panting, tears staining his blushed cheeks. He stared at his member, which was gorged and burning as though acid had been poured on it. In the steamed mirror, Peter saw a red-faced 27-year-old as red as a newborn. The door opened, sucking a narrow shaft of the hot mist, revealing Mangianelli. He was grinning, his teeth chalk-white against his olive skin, clearly pleased with himself.

"What I tell you?" he asked. "Is it a rush or what?"

The rush subsided and Peter's breathing mercifully fell back to normal nearly as quickly as it had begun. But his chest remained sunburn-red. Mangianelli assured him it would return to normal.

"When exactly?"

"Depends on the physiology."

The Sheraton Cancun was separated from the main cluster of hotels by miles of landfill swamp and strands of brush. The beach looked like one of the airline posters that lined the halls at the reservations office where he worked. There was the sugar-white sand, the candy-blue water, and a surf-side cabana made to resemble a thatched hut. Peter was surprised to discover that he didn't mind the bland, resort atmosphere. He was grateful to be liberated from the burden of wearing a heavy winter jacket everywhere and the unconscious bracing for the cold that met him every winter morning.

The boys picked out two chaise lounges from the vast, white fleet that was moored along the hotel's shore. Annie could bake for hours on sand, but Peter had brought along a portable chess set to help combat the restlessness that beaches sometimes inspired in him. Mangianelli ordered them margaritas from a roving, middle-aged Mexican waiter with bad skin and stooped shoulders. The waiter reminded Peter of the illegals he had worked with as a VISTA volunteer in South Dallas, the largely Mexican barrio in the shadow of the city's gleaming signature tower. Peter had enlisted on a kind of mission, an impulse to give back after years of prep school and college as well as a need to do something other than just go to law school like so many of his classmates. But living on subsistence wages in a ghetto had begun to grate on him when he saw other people his age driving by in their BMWs or simply going out to dinner.

"Would you look at the mangos on that schoolgirl?" Mangianelli whispered as a well- endowed woman sauntered by their chaise lounges en route to the cabana.

"You are obsessed, Mangia."

He adjusted the plastic Ray-Bans that slid down his nose. Peter thought he looked comic in sunglasses. His dark, wet hair and receding hairline made him look like John Belushi as a Blues Brother.

"Easy for you to say. Annie has the greatest knockers in Texas. But you don't care. You're a leg man."

It was true, Peter thought. He always yearned for what he didn't have or, more precisely, for what Annie couldn't offer.

"Are you going to make a move anytime soon?" Peter said.

"Don't get all bent out of shape."

"I'm not all bent out of shape. I want to play chess," Peter complained.

"What's wrong with a little anatomical appreciation?"

"You're just looking at the menu? Or are you thinking of ordering?"

Mangianelli laughed. It was deep and infectious and made you like him or forgive almost anything. Peter had been drawn to that gregarious warmth from the beginning. They had met at a company picnic, both exiles from the Northeast who thought of Texas, and Dallas in particular, as just this side of the boonies.

"That's good, P-man. I am on a diet, but I'm hungry, too."

"Maybe Annie was right," Peter said. "You are looking for an excuse."

"P-man, you trying to tell me you suddenly don't see beautiful women?"

The chess game finally got underway and lasted through a second margarita. Peter caught a soft, pleasing buzz. Time floated along as easily and weightlessly as the puffs of clouds that occasionally drifted over the beach. The hot sun and the steady drone of the surf kneaded his body, massaging away his restlessness.

"Never ceases to amaze me how we can just hop on a plane and go wherever we want," Mangianelli said. "It would be tough to give up non-revenue flying, just showing that airline card and being handed a boarding pass, gratis."

"Who's planning on giving it up?" Peter said. "C'mon, make your move."

Mangianelli's face looked uncharacteristically solemn.

"Leslie thinks I should get out of catering and go do something with the suits at HQ."

"You're a food man."

"But the money is at HQ."

"She's really working on you," Peter snapped, immediately regretting it. He worked hard to conceal his dislike of Leslie, who he believed was one of those flight attendants who worked the airlines looking for a loaded, high-flying mate. She was tall and gorgeous with a sexy mane of curly blonde hair. But he saw her as too conventionally ambitious for Mangianelli, whose passion was the art and color of food presentation. It was a rare and special enthusiasm, too—one that had forever changed how Peter himself looked at a salad in a fine restaurant. Look at the colors, look at the colors, his friend would always point out as if they were in an art gallery.

"No," Mangianelli said, picking up his bishop and sending it across the board to kill Peter's rook. "It just comes up when we talk about the future. Check."

The future, Peter mused. Why do women always want assurance about the future?

"Bastard," Peter said. "I didn't even see that coming."

"Too slow, P-man. Tequila's got your brain," he laughed.

After Mangianelli won, both settled into the environment. Peter drifted off into a sweet, welcome nap. As he did, he wondered absently why he was rarely this relaxed on a beach with Annie.

Mangianelli suddenly jumped up from the chaise lounge, startling Peter out of his breezy cocoon of sun and briny air.

"I'll be back, P-man," Mangianelli said. "I'm going to go up to the room and give Leslie a call."

"She's got you on a short leash."

"Nobody's got me on a leash."

Peter nodded and started to roll his neck to relieve the stiffness. He noticed most people were leaving the beach, heading for showers or more drinks inside the Sheraton's expansive bar. He thought of following them or being thoughtful like Mangianelli and calling Annie. But it was too soon to call; he hadn't been away even a day.

Mangianelli was gone for a long time, enough for the sun to turn from pink to a tropical tangerine, making the sand glow like smooth, bronzed skin. Peter was startled to have his view of the water suddenly blocked. A woman rose up from the sand, stretched her long thin arms, and yawned. Her sheer green robe fluttered in the breeze like a veil. Her green bikini was smooth and taut. As if following a script, the woman untied the robe and let it unfurl like a loose sail.

"I thought I was the only one out here," Peter said, bounding out of his chaise lounge. He pretended to be strolling to the water.

The woman had an easy smile that spread across a narrow, pretty face dotted with freckles. Her eyes were bright and alert, a green that reminded Peter of lush, suburban lawns.

"It's my favorite time of day," she said.

"Mine too."

Peter glanced at the smooth skin of her young, lean thighs. They slipped into an easy conversation about beaches and Cancun and vacations away from Chicago. She'd seen an ad in the Oak Park shopping weekly and knew winter vacations didn't come any cheaper, especially for a graduate student. It took weeks to talk her roommate into coming along.

"What made her change her mind?"

"We went on a diet together," she said and laughed a bright, playful, thrilling laugh. How long had it been since he had been so thrilled by a woman's laugh?

They walked together towards the water's edge. The sky and sea were changing quickly. The dramatic, tangerine light of sunset burst from the horizon and spread across the calm, indigo sea. Peter felt the simple thrill of watching a sunset, dormant for so long, rush back in all its glory.

Mangianelli was sprawled on one of the double beds, watching a movie on HBO when Peter hurried into the room. A tumbler, empty except for ice cubes and a lime wedge, sat on the night table beside him. In his hands was another margarita, its lips smudged with salt.

"You get lost?" Mangianelli asked.

"Mangia. We got any plans for dinner?" Peter was full of energy.

"You do, it looks like."

When Peter asked how he felt about having dinner with a woman from Chicago named Lauren and her friend, Rita, Mangianelli fell uncharacteristically silent. He glanced away from the TV and studied Peter with a thoughtful, bemused gaze.

"We going to need some niacin?"

"It's not about getting laid," Peter said.

"Oh," Mangianelli said, doubtfully. "You don't look like you need niacin anyway."

The taxi took the foursome through the outskirts of downtown Cancun, a dirt barrio of shacks, old tires, and strips of corrugated tin. The fading light hid the poor residents in heavy shadow except for a short, emaciated Indian woman who ambled between the shacks like a stray dog. Peter noticed her turn to look at their speeding taxi. Her dark, Mayan eyes blazed with a strange, haunting intensity.

"This a four-star restaurant we're going to?" Mangianelli joked from the other side of the cab. Peter felt Lauren's warm, soft thigh press against his when she laughed. The smell of her sultry perfume made him conjure that sheer green robe on the beach. It was like a pop song he couldn't get out of his head.

The black outlines of trees and palmettos soon appeared at the end of the long, barren road. There were low-slung cement houses with dark windows, as if they were abandoned. Headlights bounced along a narrow boulevard just beyond them. The taxi driver dropped the Americans in front of an open-air restaurant with orange plastic lanterns dangling from the wood rafters.

Absently, Peter took Lauren's hand. The warmth, the silken ease of her delicate fingers surprised and excited him. It was a cool night, and the stars spread above them like granules of white sand. The cheap lanterns gave the porch a festive village charm.

"This place is so wonderfully kitschy," Lauren gushed after the waiter had delivered the first liter of frozen margaritas.

"A toast!" Peter said, smiling at the surprise that lit Mangianelli's dark, amused eyes. He held up his smudged tumbler and turned his gaze to the faint sickle of the moon. "To new friends and the new moon."

"All right!" Mangianelli boomed. "Let the good times roll."

Lauren's pretty, delicate face shone with the afterglow of the day's hot sun. Her lips, her smooth, narrow shoulders, the graceful fingers that brushed Peter's in languid, teasing strokes under the table, all making each charged moment significant. After Lauren stood up and strolled inside the restaurant to find the restrooms, Peter found even her girlish, pigeon-toed walk to be charming and sexy.

Peter sank back in the plastic chair, buzzing with contentment. Mangianelli and Lauren's girlfriend, Rita, had drawn closer to one another.

"The secret to mole sauce is the mix of peppers, not the chocolate. Hell, you could use Hershey's if you wanted to," Mangianelli was saying. "Not that I would. But you have to be very careful to use only the best, plumpest habanero and serrano peppers."

"Hot but not overpowering," Rita offered.

"Yes. Yes. It's about balance, not power."

Peter smiled, admiring his friend's easy, gregarious charm. He was so happy about his decision to join Mangia for the weekend, absently wondering why he had ever hesitated. Annie was just jealous of his freedom. Like girlfriends before her, Peter suspected she wanted to control him, to change something about him that was more in line with who she wanted him to be.

Lauren returned, her long hair smoother from a fresh brushing and her lips moist with a new layer of balm. Peter was bursting with sweet anticipation. He loved women. Her eyes were clear and young and untroubled and they gleamed under the delicate screen of her long eyelashes. Her small, aquiline nose looked sculptural in the light and shadow. Her lips were painted with an expertly applied layer of the waxy balm and seemed to glow like her cheeks under the amber fiesta lanterns.

But when she turned briefly and smiled affectionately at him, Peter felt a disturbing, unanticipated shock. It was an un-summoned, unwanted memory. But there it was. A familiarity in Lauren's pose, a vivid recognition that he had seen it before, a cherished time that he thought was long buried and forgotten.

Annie had sat in just this same position at a café table that looked over the dark Gulf in Corpus Christi. Even the air was ripe with the same smell of the sea. She was listening to a stranger from an adjoining table. It was only their second or third date. A candle floated in a kitschy dish between them, the buttery light flickering, bathing Annie's girlish beauty, more alluring in that soft living portrait than any woman he had ever known.

Peter shook off the memory like a bad dream. How twisted, he reprimanded himself. He let himself run his fingers over Lauren's warm girlish hands, coaxing himself back into the moment.

The foursome got crazy drunk on the margaritas. Mangianelli kept ordering pitchers of the stuff and no one objected. A taxi finally drove them back through the dark barrio to the secluded beauty of the Sheraton. It was early, still, too early, Peter thought, to end the night when you were on vacation.

Mangianelli came up with the idea of the whirlpool. They started with bathing suits. Lauren wore her green bikini. Within a short time, however, the four lounged naked in the bubbling white water. Rita had brought along a bottle of tequila from her room. Peter and Mangianelli shared a conspiratorial glance. They pretended that this was utterly spontaneous, a pure and natural development they had never yearned for nor imagined. At the same time, there was an immediate understanding transmitted in that glance, a bond of silence.

Peter kissed Lauren gently, liking the smooth, anonymous warmth of the stranger's lips. There was a faint taste of the sea on them, and he closed his eyes picturing the woman in green on the beach. He kept his eyes closed tightly, forcing himself to be in the moment, to not feel what his memory had shown him at the dinner table. He pulled the woman closer, and they clung to each other in the frothing water. Lauren's thin body felt warm and pliant against his, and he knew there was no doubt that they would make love, possibly here in this whirlpool.

But the excitement didn't catch, and he could feel the passion ebbing quickly. When Peter opened his eyes, Lauren's face was bright red, as if it had been niacin induced. She looked at him, alarmed and confused at why he had stopped what he was doing. Peter stared. Her body looked gangly and awkward without the green veil. Her breasts had hard, dark nipples that turned purple in the scalding water. He closed his eyes, as if this would somehow stop the feeling that now had taken over him.

"What's wrong?" she asked.

Peter tried to answer but caught himself.

Lauren slowly fished the wet strips of rayon from the water, stepped into her green bikini, and tied on the green top.

"Too bad," Lauren said icily. "I think I'll go back to my room."

In the morning, Peter awoke to an empty room. His skull ached, and he was afraid of getting sick. It wasn't until he had dragged himself into the bathroom and splashed cold water into his puffy face and scratchy eyes that he realized Mangianelli's bed was untouched.

After a few cups of black coffee and some dry scrambled eggs stuffed into a tortilla, Peter donned his sunglasses and strolled out to the beach. It was midday and every chaise lounge was taken. He wandered through the white maze of chairs, inhaling the smells of coconut oils and sunscreens. Plastic tumblers, tinted lime-green with margaritas, dotted the white sand. He looked for Mangianelli. But it was Lauren he found. She wore a milk-white bikini, lips glistening, an empty can of Perrier in her small hand. He felt foolish that things had ended so coolly in the hot tub.

"You haven't seen my roommate?"

"They're sleeping," Lauren answered. Peter thought he saw the hint of a sardonic smile on the edge of her wet lips. Mirror sunglasses hid her eyes and reflected his own tired face. Peter's head started to throb.

"I'm sorry about what happened last night."

"It's funny," she answered after a long, uncomfortable pause. "I have a boyfriend back in Chicago. We've been together for almost a year. I'm not sure if it's going to be a permanent thing, but I've never cheated on him. I wasn't even interested in doing anything with you. I'm not sure what that was about. I guess I got caught up in the moment."

"Why didn't he come with you?"

"Tom doesn't like the beach. And he hates crowds. It would have been pure torture for him. Not that it wouldn't have been nice if he tried."

A cool breeze whisked across the beach, fluttering the umbrellas and carrying a strong scent of brine. Pop music from the surf-side bar played over the soft drone of the breakers.

"I'm not a beach person either."

"No?" Lauren laughed. "So I can only guess what brought you here."

"My friend," Peter said. "Mangianelli had been talking about a boys' weekend."

"So you both have girlfriends?" Lauren said, shaking her head. "Men."

"It's all pretty ugly, I guess."

"I just don't understand guys," Lauren said, shading the sun with her hand as she tried to find Peter's eyes behind his sunglasses.

"They're either cads or romantics."

Peter took off his glasses as if to respond but merely shrugged. He wished things had gone differently. He wished he were different. But what went through his mind was that seaside restaurant with Annie. They had just met. Everything was ahead of them. That night the air had been as soft and magical as it had when Lauren and he first arrived at the Mexican restaurant. There was the same unblemished thrill of sharing their best selves, the sudden awareness—or hope—that his future might well be poised on the other side of the flickering candle.

"It doesn't matter," Lauren said. "Take a seat if you want."

Peter sat down on the hot, white chaise beside her. Lauren observed him with what he could feel was a patient amusement.

"Well, you're not a cad."

"No," Peter said. "Not yet."

THE CAPTAIN

I.

Warrior Base, Haiti

A votive candle flickered at the captain's knees, barely illuminating the tabletop brass Buddha he had bargained from a street vendor in Bangkok. The captain wriggled his fingers, then rolled his thick neck in a wide, limp circle, the muscles crackling like bits of wood in a fire. Next, he took a deep, deliberate breath that filled out his loose-fitting combat fatigues like a balloon. He leaned far over his crossed legs, bowing humbly to the statuette as he had done weekly to a hanging Jesus when he was a boy, kneeling respectfully in the church pew alongside his devout father. *Om mani padme hum, Om mani padme hum, Om mani padme hum.* Three times he murmured the ancient mantra, the six syllables invoking compassion for all living things.

When he allowed his half-closed eyes to open fully, he met the diminutive Buddha's calm, accepting gaze, the feminine eyes that saw past postures, roles, and military rank. The enigmatic lips, hinting at a smile, struck him now as something of a parting salute.

The captain found the round, shaving mirror that dangled from the cracked cinder block next to his bunk. He inspected himself as if he were preparing to meet the Commander-in-Chief. He checked that his BDU was crisply pressed, his black leather belt smartly clamped, and, as always, he paid particular attention to his square-toed boots.

He was proud to see the russet leather gleaming like polished onyx. An officer who didn't take care of his shoes, his father often said, was likely to be a soldier who couldn't take care of himself.

As soon as he slipped on his black beret, sweat glistened from his prominent cheekbones and high, Slavic forehead, a face that he understood echoed the cherished photographs of his father as a captain in World War II. The captain felt certain his father would approve of what he had resolved to do, would understand—as few career military men would—that a soldier sometimes needed to act alone, to obey a higher code.

The dank Haitian air, as lifeless as the bald, treeless hills that surrounded the military compound, smelled like Africa. Haiti, he had found, was more African than Caribbean, more mysterious, frustrating, and thoroughly hopeless than the DR or any of the surrounding Latin islands. Haiti was tribal, consumed with secrecy, paranoia, and violence. In some ways it reminded him of Mogadishu, especially those first nights when he was just getting to know the crowded, chaotic city, and the Rangers had yet to arrive in Somalia. He was alone, wandering the streets, fighting off the hordes of desperate beggars who swirled about the American black beret like flocks of hungry pigeons.

The M16 he slung on his shoulder had been a last-minute decision. He had thought to travel unarmed, but the island was still too unpredictable.

The Army tacitly admitted to the danger with its policy of banning any soldier from the street without armored escort. But the captain had to suspend this rule, as he would have to ignore others if he was going to make a difference. Another time he might have looked the other way, pretended the treatment of Haitian "prisoners" wasn't his concern. But as one hot, muggy, mosquito-infested day dissolved into the next, it became unbearable to watch his fellow soldiers march mindlessly past the soot-covered walls of the Penitencier. They didn't know that just beyond them, just inside those old, slave walls, Haitians were still being beaten until blood leaked out with their feces and made to live in it for months. But his soldiers didn't know because General Bragg didn't want them to know. Protecting the local populace wasn't part of the military mission—whatever that was. No one really knew. It was all more than the captain could take. He was getting to know the Haitians. They were smart, industrious, caring. *Tout moun se moun,* the Haitians were fond of saying. *Tout moun se moun.* We are all human beings.

The captain slipped quietly out of the rear of the barracks. He had considered marching to the front gate and informing the guards on duty that he had to undertake immediate reconnaissance around the perimeter of the base, a half truth they might not have questioned. He had long ago developed an uncanny ability to deceive in the name of gathering useful intelligence.

The captain followed the gravel path that led behind the makeshift storage sheds. He was careful to muffle each step, knowing that sound carried far in this open, treeless countryside and could alert the young GIs. He listened to their banter recede behind him, as he made his way to a poorly lit section of the compound fence. One of the boys laughed in a way that made him envious. He'd never experienced that sense of camaraderie. Most of his career in Intel had kept him isolated from the regular movement of his peers.

The captain moved deftly into the shadows and clutched the concertina wire with his gloves, expertly avoiding the razor-sharp corners, and pulled himself up, wincing at the creak that echoed over the compound. He knew that if he was stopped, there would be no second chance.

The captain continued climbing until he reached the top and then swung himself over the rolled wire and blades that capped the fence like tumbleweed. He landed squarely in the dank mud and immediately ran toward where he knew the road to be. As soon as he felt the hard pavement underneath him, he crouched down and cleaned off his shoes with a handkerchief he'd brought for the purpose. Satisfied, he tossed the rag on the dark road and walked in the direction of the city. The only detail he hadn't worked out was exactly how he was going to get himself transported the five miles into Port-au-Prince.

II.

He watched her draw the outline first. She clutched the peppermint crayon with three fingers, as though she feared someone might pluck it away at any moment if she weren't careful. As stick trees began to sprout in the middle of her green outline, Captain Pratka studied his young daughter's face, especially the intense concentration that was undoubtedly a family trait. Like Bulldogs was the phrase that other Army brats had used to describe the Pratka kids as long as he could remember.

"What are you drawing, Katie?" he asked in a gentle, fatherly tone of voice.

"Hades," she said and reached for a brown crayon from the yellow cardboard box on their kitchen table.

"Where?"

"Hades. The country they're sending you to this time."

"Haiti. It's Haiti," Captain Pratka said, smiling. "I trust it's not Hades."

"Why not?" his daughter shot back. She was quick like her mother.

"Hades is a word for hell, Katie. That's why."

"They sound the same."

"They're not the same," Captain Pratka said firmly. The front door slammed shut like an exclamation point. He listened to his ex-wife's shoes click loudly against the linoleum floor. Not long ago that was a sound full of happy expectation. Back then he would see her glide into the kitchen, happy to be home. Now it was merely a signal that his time was just about up.

"Hi, honey bun," she said to their daughter as she stepped into the kitchen. She kissed her on the cheek almost, he thought, like an animal marking territory.

"Hi, Mommy," she said.

"What have you and Daddy been up to?" she asked. His ex-wife still hadn't extended a greeting. Nine years of marriage and it was clear she didn't even like to look at him anymore.

"Nothing," Katie said, her brown eyes a dazzling replica of her mother's, smiling at him.

"Just sharing some time before I ship off," Captain Pratka said.

"The Boys don't keep it a secret anymore?" she asked.

"Even CNN knows we're going to Haiti," he said. "The only secret is what the hell we're gonna do there."

"Operation Restore Democracy," his wife said emphatically.

It's the poorest country in the Western Hemisphere, Pratka wanted to scream. How do you bring democracy to a ghetto? But he remained silent, burying his own personal feelings about the mission. It wasn't his place to question orders or missions. He also knew his ex was likely to use his own doubts against him. She had long ago decided he wasn't the equal of intel officers like Becker, his West Point classmate who never questioned anything, greasing his way from one promotion to the next.

Pratka sometimes wished he had played the game more. But when he was younger, he had resolved to do everything on his own without any help or favors. He wanted to be self-made, to earn anything he achieved like his dad. He was only too happy to be an island on to himself.

"I guess I'll be going," Pratka said abruptly. When neither his daughter nor his wife immediately objected, he laughed nervously. "Don't miss me."

"Daddy, I'll miss you," his daughter cried, and Pratka beamed at her. She simply loved without condition.

"Be safe, Frank," his wife chipped in, finally, with a grudging conciliation. "And please, for your daughter's sake, don't try to be a hero."

"Why not, Mommy?"

"Heroes don't come home from wars, sweet pea," his wife said.

III.

Captain Pratka found the old man about a half-mile from the compound. He slouched across the open field, balancing a rusted machete on his shoulder like a rifle, oblivious to the presence of foreign soldiers and even the distant spotlights that marked the heliport, where an occasional Apache assault helicopter would rattle over the patchwork crops. Pratka approached him anyway, desperate to find a ride into the city before he was discovered by the next US patrol rumbling down the highway.

The old man bared his yellow teeth like an ill-tempered dog when Pratka greeted him, using the Haitian Creole he'd been teaching himself.

"Como ye?"

The farmer squinted at the blanc captain in full-dress uniform, one eye peeled at the M16 barrel that jutted alongside his wet face. Pratka could smell the old man's fear. Haitians had long, bitter experience with both blancs and men in military uniform and knew that their appearance was always to be feared. Pratka remembered the first reports he'd received about Titayen, the desolate marshland that served as the dumping ground for the rotting corpses that had been shot or had their throats cut by the Haitian secret police, the so-called Macoutes.

Pratka assured the old man as best he could, given the limitations of his Creole, that he was an American soldier, not a Haitian officer. He was a member of the armed forces sent by President Clinton to prepare the way for the return of Jean-Bertrand Aristide, the former slum priest who had become the popular Haitian leader—in exile. The elites, and especially the ruling drug dealers like Cedras who were nominally in power, didn't want the little bespectacled priest anywhere near their island, let alone in charge.

"Aristide!" the old farmer repeated with sudden animation. The old man, like most of Haiti's poor, dreamed of the return of their popularly elected President, a former priest who had long championed the poor.

Pratka explained that he required immediate transportation into downtown Port-au-Prince.

The old farmer waved one of his thin, emaciated arms and explained that he did not have a car, but that his nephew did. There were a few squat bungalows farther down the road, and he would find the nephew there.

"*Ou est-ce que vous allez?*" Pratka asked, suddenly abandoning the people's Creole for the French language of the ruling elite, a tactic he'd been told frightened, or at least intimidated, many of the Haitians in the impoverished countryside. He was suspicious that the old farmer was simply trying to get rid of him.

"*Voici, voici,*" the farmer said, anxiously pointing to a dilapidated shack at the edge of the distant field.

As the captain double-timed down the road, he hoped the old man was telling him the truth. It was hard to know. But he had no choice but to move forward, to complete the mission he had created for himself. He reminded himself that he had tried the official channels, presented the case to generals, but he was dismissed by the powerful, reminded again and again that he was just another enlisted man, a lowly captain at that, even after a lifetime spent in the Army.

Rank meant nothing to him now. It was action that mattered, regardless of the risks. He could be jailed or even court-martialed for doing this on his own. But so be it. He'd thought about it. But he was almost fifty years old. Time was running out. His father's advice had always been that a man should spend as much time as possible weighing a decision, but once the decision was made, there had to be complete commitment. There could be no hesitation, no holding back. In battle, death followed doubt.

The captain was relieved to see the outlines of the wood shacks appear at the crest of the hill. There was an old Nissan pickup truck parked next to one of them, its back window busted. As he came closer he glimpsed a small, muddy pen with one scrawny chicken poking around a mound of trash. Food continued to be scarce in Haiti, despite the presence of the US, another fact of Operation Restore Democracy that Pratka found to be poorly planned. There was no reason the Army couldn't make some effort to get these people the basics.

The nephew appeared from inside the bungalow, clearly having been tipped off. The rest of his family had vanished silently into the night. These people are good at hiding, Pratka acknowledged. The nephew, a gangly teenager with a quick, warm smile, was only too happy to drive him into Port-au-Prince. For a fee.

"You're looking for action, General?" the teenager asked, lowering his voice to a conspiratorial tone. "Jean Phillipe knows where to take you. And no one will know," Jean Phillipe said. "Your secret will be safe with me."

"I'll give you thirty dollars," Captain Pratka said.

"Fifty US is the going rate," Jean-Phillipe said.

Pratka liked the boy's cockiness. Any show of courage encouraged more of the same.

A few minutes later Jean-Phillipe was gunning his battered Datsun pickup down the road, windows open to the soft night air.

"We have friends following us."

Pratka glanced through the broken cab window behind him. The small, round lights were barely visible through the shards of glass held together with duct tape.

"American?" Jean-Phillipe asked.

Pratka shook his head. They were local. Army was not allowed to go anywhere without the blazing lights of a Humvee escort.

"Are you sure?" Jean-Phillipe asked, his eyes showing fear for the first time.

"They don't concern us. If they know what's good for them."

"Unless they are Macoutes."

"There is nothing to fear from them."

"You do not know the Macoutes," Jean-Phillipe said.

Pratka had learned enough to know how deeply feared they were throughout the country. They were more than ruthless. They had acquired a mythical aura, unstoppable, evil spirits that roamed the country with an unquenchable thirst for blood. In fact, they were simply hit men, professionals who spread terror to pacify any would-be political opposition.

"You don't know what kind of Army is protecting your country,

Jean-Phillipe. Any threat will be met swiftly and with extreme prejudice."

"And after I drop you off?" Jean-Phillipe asked. When he checked the rearview mirror, the white jeep was still there, its reflection shimmering in the dark glass like a ghost.

"You Americans have much faith in your army."

"It's the finest in the world."

"Then why are you running from it?"

Pratka shot a hostile glance at the boy.

"I'm warning them," he said finally. "I'm warning the Army of the Trojan Horse that threatens to undermine all that we do."

"Huh?"

"It's from an ancient Greek story about war. A priest named Laocoon tried to warn his army of their willful ignorance, but they would not listen."

"Oh. OK," the boy's voice drifted off, his tone less sure, as if he might be talking to a *fol*, a crazy.

The Datsun rumbled over the potholed road toward the black harbor. There were no boats in sight except for the tower lights on the US Navy destroyer docked far across the Bay. As they came closer, Pratka noted the bone-white sliver of moon painted on the still water. The Buddhist prayer swirled in his mind, a chant he had repeated often.

Thus shall ye think of this fleeting world:
A star at dawn, a bubble in a stream;
A flash of lightning in a summer cloud;
A flickering lamp, a phantom, and a dream.

"This is good," Pratka ordered. "Let me off here."

The captain pulled himself out of the pickup and onto the empty street. Except for a skeleton-thin dog sniffing the wet gutter, nothing stirred. A strict curfew forbid anyone to be on the streets after nightfall. Pratka checked for Army patrols before he took his hand off the hood. He'd made it this far, and he didn't want to be detected so close to his destination.

"Know where you're going?" Jean-Phillipe said with a quick grin.

Pratka backed away from the car and gave Jean-Phillipe a half salute. At that moment he remembered an uncannily similar scene. He was 18, about to leave home for good, and his father had given him a brief, formal salute good-bye. That was all. No hug, no expression of affection. His father didn't trust emotions. "If you don't control them, they control you," was his frequent advice to his only son. "That's your weakness, young man. You're impatient, and you lose control."

Pratka didn't know if he believed his professed dictum about emotions, even though the old man made it difficult to read what he was really feeling at any given moment. His own sensitivity to others made Pratka suspect that his ideas were a bluff, a way to protect whatever it was that raged inside him.

Regardless, Pratka had learned to respond to his father's distance with quiet acquiescence. He accepted his father's stoicism as the price of being part of a military family. Pratka was from a long line of career soldiers, each more decorated than the last. From the Civil War, when his great-grandfather served the Union, to his own father's participation in the Great War, his family had answered the call of duty.

"Be careful," Pratka said to the boy. He was startled to hear his voice echo with the rare but familiar resonance of his father, a voice he assumed was silenced in the depths of Arlington National Cemetery. But here it was, issuing from the grave and through him like *vodou* spirits.

Pratka watched the pickup's red taillights drift down the block, sorry to see the boy go. He waited until the red taillights sailed into the distance and then disappeared altogether.

The captain crouched in the shadow of the *Penitencier's* awning, listening to the approaching footsteps, judging both their speed and size by the depth of the sound they created on the wet concrete. The man was small and slight, and his steps carried the scrape and click of civilian leather shoes. The man walking toward him was not a guard or a soldier, since both wore cheap boots that slapped the pavement like tennis shoes. Pratka, himself, stood in his bare feet, so as not to make any sound at all.

The civilian steps stopped abruptly in front of the door, a thick key zipped inside the deep lock and clicked over the heavy bolt. As the door's heavy, rusted hinges creaked, Pratka darted out of his hiding place and slipped inside the closing crack, just paces behind the small man. Immediately, Pratka ran soundlessly to a dark corner, keeping his eyes pinned on the figure scraping up the stairs above him. A moment later he recognized that the civilian was the warden himself.

Pratka ran up the steps without making a sound and arrived alongside the warden just as he was walking down a dark corridor.

"Keep moving," the captain ordered, pushing the barrel into the warden's back. The Haitian remained strangely calm, his smooth, coal-black face not showing the least surprise when they finally arrived at his office. The captain announced that he had come to inspect the prison.

"Without orders, I can do nothing," the warden said, standing next to his fine, wood desk, his chalk-white eyes serene behind the tortoiseshell glasses.

"I'm ordering you."

The Haitian nodded respectfully. "Under whose authority?"

"Mine."

The captain pointed his gun barrel back toward the door. The warden shrugged and led him through the hallway before they clamored down the cement steps to the first holding block. Even before they reached the barred gate, the stench of shit and urine burned his nose. The ammonia alone made him gag. Throngs of bare-chested Haitians were clustered near the iron-gated door, their dark skin gleaming like wet blacktop in the harsh spotlights that leaked through the one high, barred window. His intelligence reports had been all too accurate. There were scores of men crammed into a cell meant for five.

"How long have they been incarcerated?" Pratka asked.

"All different. As their crimes are," the warden said, folding his hands under his arms in a Napoleonic stance.

"All have been convicted?"

"No."

"And those men. How long?"

"A few months. Perhaps longer in some cases."

"You're not sure? You don't know how long your own charges have been incarcerated?"

Pratka bristled with anger, indignant at the casualness of this cruelty. No one was respected. No one mattered.

"As you can see, there are many."

The warden's round, placid face remained unperturbed. The captain had to fight his instinct to strike the man, to break that pose of detachment he knew so well, had lived around his entire life.

"You have written records. Documents."

"In my office."

"Good. We'll have a look. Then I want you to call my commanding officer."

"I don't understand, sir."

"You will."

IV.

Pratka stood at attention alongside the warden's desk, cradling his M16 when the US Military Liaison Officer marched through the door. Colonel Becker. Of course, Pratka mused as he struggled to hide his shock. Lieutenant Major Tom Becker. West Point. His ex-wife's poster boy for the Army.

"What's going on here?" the lawyerlike colonel asked. The warden, who sat stiffly behind his desk, turned to face the captain. Pratka's plan had been to lure his own reluctant Army into the prison, so that they would be forced to witness the conditions and do something about it.

"Pratka?" Becker started. The expression on his face added, "What the hell?"

They'd last spoke at the first intel briefing, hours after the soft invasion was complete. Becker had given a smart, articulate report about drug operatives in Haiti. There was nothing new in the report, nothing that couldn't have been found in The New York *Times*. Everyone was well aware that Cedras and a host of other top Haitian officials were deeply involved in the coca trade—but Becker's delivery, as neat and tied up as his pressed uniform, impressed the Command.

Pratka assumed the same tone as an intel report when he finally spoke.

"The prisoners present in this facility are being subjected to cruel and unusual punishment, sir. In flagrant violation of all existing international laws and covenants governing treatment of the incarcerated," Pratka said. "I requested the warden, here, to contact you and a protection unit to come here."

"Pratka. Is this some kind of reconnaissance? Because if it is…"

"No. I'm on my own."

"I don't get it."

"You will. Something needs to be done, and it was incumbent upon me to give the Army a little shove."

Becker turned slightly askance, the way characters did in movies, not in real life, as if to give Pratka a chance to admit he had been drinking or even sampled some of the ganja that was easier to find than food on the island.

"There's nothing wrong with me," Pratka said. He began to hear himself speak, as though he were a character, apart from the reality in front of them.

"I reported this *Penitencier* to authorities, and all claimed it was none of mine or the Army's business."

"Who sent you here?" Becker continued, still struggling to understand what was going on.

"I told you, Becker. No one."

"No one."

Pratka nodded.

"I observed those prisoners in the cell containment area. All are emaciated and exhibit other signs of ill treatment," Pratka said.

"Cut it out, Pratka. This has Special Ops stupidity all over it. Tell me whose mission idea this was."

"President Clinton. You heard the speech. The President said we were to free the people of Haiti from all forms of repression, and establish the political atmosphere necessary for democracy."

"Politicians always say crap like that."

"Sir, as a United States officer, I am under oath to uphold the orders of the Commander- in-Chief."

"You're under oath to the US Army, Captain, to the US Constitution, and yes, to the Commander-in-Chief. But be a looney. You can take this whole lark up with Bragg, not me," he said.

"I did that, sir."

"What?" Becker was honestly surprised. "So, what are you doing here?"

"General Bragg said the mission was force protection. We came here to look after our own asses. We were not to interfere with Haitian-on-Haitian violence."

"Those ARE the orders."

"Becker. These people are being tortured while we babysit."

"This whole mission is a crock, Captain. That's no secret. But we have orders."

"Go and take a look, sir. They're ankle-deep in their own shit. They have no food or water. Many have open wounds already pussed with infection. Few have even committed a crime other than being out of favor of the regime. It's criminal, sir."

"Maybe it is. I've been ordered to come here and take care of YOU."

"I don't need help. They do."

"We're not cops. We're soldiers."

"If we're not here to help these people, what are we doing?"

"That's not up to you. We obey orders. That's it. That's the whole code."

Becker folded his arms slowly as if he were preparing to give a lecture.

"You and I both know this is one fucked-up country. It's been fucked up, and it's always going to be fucked. Why do you think it's the poorest goddamn piece of real estate in the Western Hemisphere?"

"I know the history."

"Do you? So, why are you the self-appointed liberator?"

Pratka didn't see himself this way. He was acting on what he knew and others did not. The knowledge gave him responsibility. It occurred to him, however, that he could stop what he was doing. Once the backup platoon arrived, word about this torture chamber would be out.

"Just who the hell do you think you are, Pratka?" Becker snapped. His dark blue eyes narrowed with angry frustration. "You're making yourself your own command."

The captain smiled. It had been his reaction to being reprimanded since he was a boy. The smile would infuriate whomever it fell upon. But the smile was a reflex, a response that took him deeper into himself where he could not be touched, would not suffer humiliation. As an adult, that smile was a kind of line in the sand where his innate stubbornness took over.

"You think this is some big joke, mister?" Becker said.

"No, sir. I don't," the captain said, his smile lingering.

A moment later their standoff was interrupted by the sound of combat boots clomping down the cement hallway. Half a platoon entered the tiny office, M16s drawn, ready to shoot.

"Good morning," the captain said, resting the rifle on his lap and nodding at his fellow soldiers. Only now they stared at him as they would a booby trap, fearful of touching off a deathly explosion.

V.

The sound of a milling crowd suddenly rose from the street outside his cinder block detention cell. Pratka could hear the buzz and chatter of disembodied voices growing as others joined in. He walked to the tiny, porthole window and peered through the rusted bars.

A group of Haitians had gathered alongside the water and begun to chant. Some made strange, high-pitched whining noises that sounded both funny and ominous. Vodou country. Pratka knew that many Haitians believed in all sorts of supernatural powers, finding evidence of spirits in sticks, dolls, and a sudden gust of wind. Like The Noble Teachings, they understood that the material world was insubstantial, merely the expression of a much larger existence.

In a very short time, the crowd worked itself into a frenzy. They swayed, clinging to each other, a mass of rolling, black heads and fluttering T-shirts alongside the shallow, green water. Their voices rose and fell, following a dark, hypnotic rhythm that seemed to beckon the storm clouds that approached on the horizon, billowing toward them like smoke from a raging fire.

For the first time, Pratka sensed the approaching wrath of his history, the US Army. He had defied them, and the reasons for it didn't matter. Only the arrogance of the defiance. Pratka understood he could be court-martialed now. He was like Laocoon, the Greek priest who had warned the people of Troy that their enemies were hidden inside the huge, wooden horse, plotting to sneak out under cover of night and take over the city. But no one listened to Laocoon. In a moment of rage and frustration, Laocoon hurled his spear at the belly of the huge Trojan horse. It bounced off, harmless. But the people of Troy were stung by his arrogance. They called to the gods not for protection, but for Laocoon's punishment. Soon snakes emerged. Attacking from stormy seas.

The Haitians were hysterical with their chanting, their Creole echoing over the waters like some ancient call out of Africa. *N'ap boule. N'ap boule.* We're on fire. The sour breeze blowing across the street crackled with static electricity. The chanters now had their hands in the air and were grinning, laughing, cheering on the approaching clouds. The darkness bled across the horizon, shadowing the gray sea, which flashed with white caps. There was a power, a fierce impenetrability about the advancing storm that worried Pratka. It was not the hurricane season, and there none of the brownish, swirling clouds that often preceded one. But he felt the same foreboding, the same odd and terrifying exhilaration.

Shooting Harlem

Burns worried that the apartment building looming in the blue darkness was too clean for Harlem. The security fence was new and gleamed silver under the white brilliance of the spotlights. The bushes were groomed. He could smell the fresh-cut lawn that graced the entrance. This was not the East Harlem Burns had raced through red lights to capture at magic hour.

"You got a haircut," a familiar voice drawled behind him. "Chopped off the ponytail."

"I hate when this happens, Joel. You go on location thinking you're going to create some great footage, then this. No one is going to understand this is Harlem. They're expecting a ghetto, a place to escape—not move to."

"We can make it look bad," Joel said with a smile in his dark, tired eyes. He and the video crew had been locked inside the production van for over an hour, waiting for Burns to arrive, worried they might have the wrong address.

"Everybody is getting their hair cut off now," Joel continued. "Even my son Charlie wants to be bald, and the kid's only ten."

"I'm not bald," Burns said. His once thick, black hair was thinning, a development he feared was a sign that he was aging fast, too fast for the youthful world of TV news.

"If you say so. Now what do we want out of Harlem?"

Burns turned to get a better view of the surrounding neighborhood. Immediately, he was drawn to the raised subway platform at the distant end of the street. The narrow platform perched uneasily on the summit of the towering black trestles.

"That's the kind of thing we're going to need," Burns said.

"It looks pretty bad," Joel said, turning back to the van. "I'll get it set up."

As the crew unpacked the camera and equipment, Burns watched a subway car rattle onto the platform where commuters huddled under the sulfurous haze of the station lights. They appeared gray and indistinct, like characters glimpsed in a morning fog. Burns guessed the IRT would ferry them to midtown, where they would become part of that invisible army of doormen, security guards, clerks and telephone operators that kept the city running. They barely earned enough money to stay off the streets and probably never enough to move away. They were the permanent underclass, Burns thought, trapped on a treadmill, a never-ending circle of near poverty. What hope did they have? They were born into it much the way he was born into privilege and opportunity.

But as he watched the commuters squeeze inside the train, Burns remembered racing down the hallway with his executive producer. Katz was hurrying to yet another meeting and had ordered Burns to walk him there. He never liked to let Burns forget who was in charge.

"This is a story about a Harlem school girl who gets a college scholarship and a ticket out of the ghetto," Katz had said. "Make sure you bring me back some characters. People we want to cheer for."

"But there's something off here," Burns said. "These kids don't get their money until they're old enough for college. That's almost twelve years. Long time in a place like Harlem."

"Get your Emmy for the next one," Katz said. "This is a feel-good piece. Nothing ambitious."

"But this Wall Street Foundation comes off looking like the white knight with some shaky promises. No cash. You know the deal is that if the kids don't make it through those twelve years, they don't get the money. Not a penny, Katz. The whole thing hits me more like a PR stunt than trying to save Harlem."

Katz stopped abruptly in the hallway. His gray eyes were cool with anger and Burns knew that his boss would welcome an excuse to fire him. They didn't see stories the same way.

"An intern could do this piece, Burns. If you can't handle it the way it should be handled, tell me now."

A bored Dominican guard sat inside the bullet-proof, Plexiglas security booth, a row of black and white security screens flickering behind him. He glanced at Burns and the crew without surprise or even interest, as if white television crews were always appearing at dawn in the East Harlem projects. Before Burns even spoke into the intercom, the guard buzzed them inside the building.

"Ida Murphy?" Burns asked. "She's expecting us."

"Leven Jay," the guard answered, his eyes riveted on the portable TV that sat just under his desk. Burns could hear the faint but familiar theme music of the "Today" show.

"Is there a freight elevator?" Burns asked.

The guard glanced at the flatbed cart for the first time. It was piled chest-high with heavy armored cases and loose stacks of thick aluminum poles. The guard studied the arms-like cache with the same blank intensity as the television screen, then pointed to the far elevator with a flick of his dark eyes and returned his attention to the tube.

The crew fell in line behind Burns like an army platoon marching through a village. They were jittery, anxious to work after spending so much time cooped up in the van, waiting for their producer.

"Smells like the bathroom at HoJo's, don't it?" Elf said, raising his long, sharp nose at the lobby like a connoisseur.

"It's called ammonia, Elf. It's for keeping things clean. You might try it some time," Bookman said. The rest of the crew laughed on cue at the old joke. Elf had coarse, stringy hair and an angular face ravaged by acne. He never looked clean.

"Listen to the pigs snort," Elf said, stopping in front of the elevator door.

The prime space in front of the controls was reserved for Burns, who was the last to step inside. The crew fell silent as the doors closed. Burns stared straight ahead, his stern, prominent jaw reflecting back at him from the stainless steel. He knew it was difficult to predict how any one character would react to the invasion of camera crews. Some were instantly resentful, others couldn't do enough for you. There had been something in Ida Murphy's voice on the telephone that made Burns worry that she might be one of those rare people who were not in the least intimidated by cameras and the prospect of being on TV. They expected something for their effort.

"Remember, keep it civil, boys," Burns warned after the elevator had chugged to a stop.

"Hear that, Elf?" Bookman taunted. "No flirting with the first-graders."

"Be about the right size for your dong," Elf said, helping to push the heavy equipment cart down the dim hallway.

"Cool it," Burns ordered, then hesitated in front of the apartment door. He waited for complete quiet before he finally knocked.

Mrs. Ida Murphy answered the door. The musk perfume appeared first, then a smiling, middle-aged school teacher. She was plump and overdressed in a business suit and heels. Her ample breasts swelled above her blouse.

"I know that voice from the telephone," Ida said, flashing another wide smile at Burns. "But you're a little early. We're not ready just yet."

"That's OK," Burns answered. He hesitated, feeling the same uneasiness with her that he'd sensed on the telephone. "We have to set up a few lights, anyway. If that's all right."

Mrs. Murphy didn't object when Burns stepped past her, followed by Joel, the equipment cart and the crew who strolled single file, greeting her with a respectful nod. Only Bookman broke rank after he spotted the bathroom door, hurrying past Ida's daughters, who hid in the corner of the small, dark dining room. Their wide eyes followed Burns as he scouted the adjacent living room where morning cartoons chirped from a giant screen television.

"Looks like an apartment in Queens," Joel said.

Burns hurried ahead, his disappointment rising as he noted the plush blue carpet, the freshly shined mahogany furniture, the antique mirror that hung tastefully over a modern sofa.

"Since when did they start making apartments like this in Harlem?" Burns whispered. "Hell, I'd be lucky to have an apartment like this."

"Nice tube," Joel said, admiring the giant Sony that dominated the room.

"Is there something wrong, Mr. Burns?" Ida Murphy asked, sauntering in from the kitchen.

"Not a thing," Burns said. "Nice place you have here.

The flush of a toilet roared through the apartment. A moment later, Bookman stumbled out of the bathroom and into the hallway. Elf snickered as he continued to unravel an audio wire.

"Ain't nobody going near that room for awhile," Elf said.

As the crew dragged the video equipment off the cart, Burns huddled in the corner with Joel, discussing cutaways, scenes that could be used to cover voice-over narration or bits of the interview. Cutaways were almost always staged, innocent re-creations of someone taking a walk or watching television or talking on the telephone. But Burns wanted to try something different, a lighting scheme that would make the apartment seem a little less affluent.

"You got to go one way or the other, Burns," Joel whispered. "You either shoot this stuff as stark or you shoot like it is. If we light dim, it'll just come out like bad lighting. It'll look like you just had a lousy cameraman who didn't know what he was doing."

"How do you make plush carpet look stark?" Burns asked.

"Tight focus, stay away from shots of any of the good furniture, let the camera shake a little. We can try any number of things."

Burns felt Ida's eyes watching him from inside the kitchen. She was one of the nosiest characters he'd ever had to shoot.

"Let's be true to the story," Burns said.

"What's the story again?" Joel asked.

"Ghetto family makes good."

"So we're in a ghetto, right now," Joel said with an impish grin.

The first scene was the family's morning routine. Burns positioned the two girls at the kitchen table, their school books piled at one end, waiting to be rushed to school. Sandra, the first-grader who had been awarded the scholarship, crossed her legs, swinging them from the tall chair. She grinned at Burns, basking in his attention. Her older sister, Michelle, was shy and quiet but warmed up after Burns explained that both she and Sandra would be in the picture. Satisfied with the image of the sisters chatting at the breakfast table, Burns then asked Ida to follow her usual habits as if the camera wasn't there.

"We just want to see a normal morning at the Murphy home."

Ida nodded, then sauntered into the kitchen. She yanked cereal boxes from the shelf, milk, orange juice, jelly and eggs from the refrigerator, bowls, cups, glasses from the new cabinets. She did everything at once then stopped, realizing she would not be able to carry all the breakfast supplies to the table. Her daughters giggled.

"That was a good start, Ida," Burns said, making himself smile.

"But if you don't mind, I'd like to try it again. This time maybe you and I could work out something simpler, easier, so that more of the attention is on you instead of the food you're getting together. Does that sound like a good idea to you?"

Ida nodded stiffly.

"Great," Burns said. "Maybe we can start with you taking the milk out of the refrigerator, then getting some bowls, then cereal. Do them one at a time, looking at your daughters each time. But don't make it too obvious. We want it to look real, natural. Exactly what you do every day."

"The Murphy Kitchen. Take One," Elf called, slating the shot on audio so that it could easily be identified when the tape was reviewed during the edit.

Ida opened the refrigerator and the kids started talking on cue. Burns was relieved that the family was able to ignore the presence of the video crew and the bright white lights that circled them. Ida set the bowls gently on the table.

"Would you girls like anything else?" Ida asked. Her daughters shook their heads and started to eat, managing to continue their conversation. Burns was amazed that Ida would be so transparently courteous. What real mother, especially a mother struggling with life in Harlem, talked to her kids like a waitress?

"Stop tape," Burns ordered. The girls stopped talking—but not eating—and Ida leaned back in her chair, exhaling slowly and carefully. The black dense hair by her forehead had flattened from the dampness.

"That was a little too studied," Burns explained, sounding like the director coaching his actress. "We have to keep this looking natural. You know what I'm saying? Imagine you're tired, overworked and not in a great mood. It's a tough morning. Got it?"

Ida sauntered back to her opening mark without complaint. The bowls were taken away and put in a box off the set. The girls remained quiet, their eyes cast down, waiting again for their cue. Elf slated the new take.

Ida delivered the cereal, her shoulders sagging slightly as if she were struggling to wake up. She returned to the kitchen for a cup of coffee, then eased into her chair, sipping silently from the steaming mug. Her daughters took turns shaking cereal from the box, chatting with one another while Mom stared into space. It was an effortlessly professional performance. But neither Burns nor his crew paid attention to the red plastic tumbler until Michelle had slipped it from under the table and held it directly in front of her face, partly obscuring her shrewd, dark eyes. 'Cornell University' was emblazoned across the cup, the letters large and as easy to read as a billboard advertisement.

"Stop tape," Burns ordered. He paused after the video recorder clicked to a stop, letting the ensuing silence gather force, using the awkwardness. "Michelle. I like the cup but it really blocks your face, which is what we all want to see."

"I want to go to Cornell," she said impulsively, tossing a quick, conspiratorial glance at her mother.

"She wants a scholarship like her sister," Ida confirmed.

"And she should have one," Burns said. "But this is news, not a commercial. We'll do this one more time but without the cup. OK, Michelle?"

"What's the harm in letting my daughter hold the cup?" Ida demanded.

Burns shook his head, wondering what was happening to his story. Maybe he should have turned it down when Katz offered.

"You keep it, Michelle," Ida said. She raised her chin and stared defiantly at Burns. Joel and the crew hesitated, watching from the shadows behind the lights like a studio audience, curious to see how the producer would handle the challenge to his authority.

Burns wanted to argue, to put this lady in her place. But he had to keep his character happy or the interview would be a bust.

"All right, all right," Burns said. "Keep the cup."

Ida was positioned on her salmon couch with a blank, featureless wall behind her. Burns wanted the lighting designed so that Ida's face was illuminated by the brittle dawn just beginning to spill through the box window. The harsh, bluish light would make Ida look tougher, more hardened than she appeared and would also create dark, defined shadows, the kind of lighting that the movies used to suggest ghetto.

"Think moody. Think shadows," Burns prodded Joel. "Think Caravaggio."

Burns had saved an article in a film magazine about a movie cameraman who spent months studying Caravaggio's paintings, planning to copy the Italian master's brilliant use of chiaroscuro in his next film. Burns liked high production values in his news reports, a holdover from a time when he thought of becoming a film maker.

"Where do you come up with all these artists no one has ever heard of?" Joel asked.

"He's famous," Burns said. "How about Rembrandt?"

"Rembrandt," Joel said, nodding. "Video Rembrandt coming right up."

Burns sat on the end of the matching love seat, facing Ida. He clasped his hands and leaned over with a studied casualness. He couldn't remember the last time he'd had to work so hard at being pleasant.

"What is it you'll be asking me?" Ida asked, glancing warily at the crew setting up lights around her. For the first time, Burns noticed the tacky gold eye shadow highlighting her round, onyx eyes.

"Nothing prying," Burns assured her. "Just your thoughts on the scholarship your little daughter has been awarded."

"I want the specific questions."

"I don't know what they are yet," Burns lied.

Ida stiffened when Bookman ran the microphone wire behind her, hiding it from the camera's view. The concealed microphone was essential to Burns. He liked the character as natural-looking as possible.

"Got to keep the wire out of view, Ma'am." Bookman explained, showing her the thimble-sized microphone. Ida stared at the tiny receiver like it was a bug.

After the lights were finally set, Burns handed Ida a pocket powder case and asked if she wouldn't mind dabbing her forehead with the absorbent pad. The heat from the quartz lamps was beginning to make her shine. Burns watched quietly as she snapped open the case and found her reflection in the small mirror. She held the wafer-thin pad between her long fingers and brushed the powder across her forehead in smooth, languid strokes. She watched herself being watched, serenely aware that she was only a physical object.

Her pose made Burns feel a sudden, unexpected empathy. She had no illusions about why she had been asked to appear on television. She knew she was playing a part, a pose demanded by others.

"Roll tape…" Burns ordered, sitting up straight.

"Rolling… Speed," Elf confirmed, talking to the digital numbers flashing on the recorder.

"How do you feel, now that your kids can leave Harlem?" Burns asked.

"We're not leaving Harlem, Mr. Burns."

"I'm sorry, Ida. I didn't mean it that way. How do you feel about the future?"

Ida, understanding and accepting her role, gave a concise testimonial, enthusing on how the college scholarship would inspire her youngest daughter to be an even better student, now that she had a goal, a bright future. It would give Sandra the opportunity to be whatever she wanted to be, provided, of course, that she worked hard.

Burns knew it was a good sound bite, exactly what Katz was looking for him to bring back. But Burns also heard Katz's condescending tone of voice telling him that an intern could produce this piece.

"Ida," Burns said, absently pressing a finger to his dimpled chin. "Does it bother you that you and your daughter will have to wait thirteen years to get this money? Do you think about what happens in the meantime?"

Ida hesitated, momentarily bewildered, like an actress being suddenly confronted with lines she had never heard before.

"Well, you know," Ida said. "This has given hope and courage to my eldest daughter, who would like to attend Cornell University. But Cornell University is very expensive. I hope and pray that we can save enough money so that Michelle can follow her own dreams."

"That's not what I asked," Burns said.

"We are appreciative of the scholarship," Ida said, folding her arms, refusing to answer.

"But it's just a piece of paper right now," Burns said. "They can find any number of reasons not to give it to you."

"It's something, Mr. Burns."

Burns hesitated, deciding whether or not to press the issue further. But he sensed that he would not get what he was after, would only embarrass this woman and himself.

"That's a wrap," Burns called to the crew. Immediately, the quartz lamps were snapped off and Burns felt himself relax into the cool shadows.

"If you'll just sign this release," Burns said, handing Ida a sheet of paper. He usually had talent sign the release before the interview, but he'd forgotten about it until now.

"What's this for?" Ida asked, trying to read the legal jargon on the release at the same time.

"It's just protection," Burns said, offering her a pen.

"From what?"

"From lawyers," Burns said, trying to make a joke.

"Lawyers?" Ida asked.

"This is routine, Ida," Burns said. "You just sign this and that allows you to be on television."

"Let me get my glasses," Ida said.

"We're on deadline," Burns said. "We don't have much time. Trust me, this is very routine."

"I don't sign nothin' till I read it. Every word."

When Ida returned, her champagne-gold reading glasses were perched on her nose in a way that made Burns think of a school marm.

"When do we see something?" Ida asked.

"I'll call you with the air date," Burns said. "As soon as I know."

"I want to see it before it's on TV," Ida said.

"That's not possible."

"Isn't there something before the video goes on TV?"

"We don't screen rough cuts," Burns said. "For one thing, they're hard to understand. They've got counter numbers in the picture and the audio isn't mixed."

"I see," Ida said, folding the release. "Then I don't know if it's exactly right to let you use us."

"We're not using you," Burns said. "We're telling your story which is a story people need to hear. It's hopeful, it promises a future. It's a way out of poverty."

"Look, honey. We make a pretty good living. I work hard for it. I want more for my children, sure, but we ain't in no poverty. Just whose story you tryin' to tell here? You think we're all just a bunch of poor dumb Uncle Toms too stupid to make a go at it?"

"I don't want to get into a racist thing here."

"Harlem is home for a lot us. Just like whatever fancy little condo you live in is. We're proud of our neighborhood."

"Of course you are. You have every right to be," Burns said.

"And I got a right to see this rough cut. I got a right to know what you're planning to do with me. This is my life, honey."

"It is policy not to show rough cuts," Burns said. "You have to understand that."

Ida nodded, waiting patiently.

"I need you to sign that release," Burns said.

Ida adjusted the glasses on her nose and unfolded the release.

"It says here that by signing I give the TV station the right to use my image any way you see fit to use it. Seems a little one-sided to me."

Burns smiled blandly. His crew was finished packing up and were pushing the equipment cart towards the door.

"You agreed to do this interview, Ida," Burns said, suppressing the anxiety that spread through him, the sense of an impending disaster. He could only imagine Katz's reaction to a story that could not legally be aired. "The release is just a formality."

"Is it? Well, then I guess we're through," she said, handing him the release. Burns stared at the paper as if it were a snake, poised to strike.

"I can't promise anything, Ida. But maybe I can call on some favors. It's highly unusual. But I think your story is too important. It needs to get on the air. People need to know about you and your daughters."

"Uh huh," Ida said, doubtfully.

"Sign the release, Mrs. Murphy," Burns insisted. "I promise you I'll get this on the air one way or the other."

"Are you threatening me?"

"I'm telling you that there is a thing called the freedom of the press. The public is entitled to know what goes on here."

"If I read this right, Mr. Burns, you don't get that freedom unless I give it to you."

Burns wanted to leave, to just walk out the door and pretend that he would put Ida on the air any way he chose. But he knew he couldn't. He knew she had the upper hand.

"I'm just trying to do my job," Burns said finally.

"Ain't we all, Mr. Burns. Ain't we all."

"So you don't mind helping me out here?"

Ida Murphy smiled and glanced away with a shyness that reminded Burns of the woman's youngest daughter, the little girl that had been awarded the scholarship.

"I just don't feel right signing without seeing everything first."

Burns's crew lingered at the door, anxious to leave.

"I'll call you," Burns said, wondering how he was going to get an arrangement like this past Katz.

"You want to take this paper with you?" Ida asked.

"No, thanks. I've got a box of blank ones in the car," Burns said, and walked off to meet his crew.

PUBLICATION
CREDITS

"Video Verite" appeared in *Confrontation*
(No. 70/71, Winter/Spring 2000, "Another Time")

"The Barrens" appeared in *The Distillery*
(Vol XIII, No. 2, Jan. 2007)

"Orange, Texas" appeared in *The Distillery*
(Vol IV, No. 1, Winter 1997)

"Car Crazy" appeared in *The Orange Willow Review*
(Vol. 2, 1999-2000)

"Crossing Water" appeared in *Palo Alto Review*
(Vol. VII, No. 2, Fall 1998)

"Sins Of The Father" appeared in *Quercus Review*
(No. 8, 2008)

"Telling Time" appeared in *Lynx Eye*
(Vol. IV, No. 1, Winter 1997)

"Turn Around" appeared in *Rivers Edge*
(Vol. 10, No. 2, Spring 1996)

"The Perfect View" appeared in *The Worcester Review*
(Vol. XXVIII, No. 1,2, 2007)

"Shooting Harlem" appeared in *Emry's Journal*
(Vol. 14, Spring 1997)